Congrats on winning. Hope you enjoy!

Scarlett

Wunderland

SCARLETT SE LEVA

Published by Bookends Publishing, Florida

Paperback ISBN: 978-1-7363934-1-3
E-book ISBN: 978-1-7363934-0-6
ASIN: B08R8J2NW7

To my three musketeers.

Prologue

I try to comprehend the words that my best friend just uttered. Flustered and filled with doubt, I stand still as I watch her fleeing in her midnight-blue sports car.

Why would she do that to me? Why? She knows what she was doing and what this information would do to me.

Why is it so hot? I swear.

Around campus, everyone wore jackets, sweaters, and coats. I could have sworn when I last checked my phone it said it was forty degrees. Why do I feel like the sun is directly pelting me?

My bra feels damp and uncomfortable. Do I have my inhaler with me? What the heck is happening?

Who would have thought this was what this day had in plan for me? *Can I get another option, Alex?*

Wait, do I really want another option? Questions upon questions come at me in lighting speed.

Get it together Simone. You have to pull yourself together. You know what you need to do to get through this. Inhale. Exhale. Repeat five more times, and then move. Who would have thought my day would go like this?

1

Chapter One

SEPTEMBER 24, 2008

I am not a morning person, to say the least. I am never at my best this early. I creep across the bedroom to the bathroom. The frigidness of the shower helps to better my somber mood.

It's September, in New York, and the weather is perfect not cold and not hot, just the right amount of crisp in the air. I pair some boots with my black skinny jeans and light gray, scoop neck sweater.

Brewed Beans Co. is my next and most important stop of the day. BB's has the moistest blueberry muffin and toe-curling mocha latte. I shouldn't be buying food from BB's; five bucks for a cup of coffee is expensive, especially on a college student's budget, but this shit is addicting.

I have a huge test, and I know that I deserve this. My budget can stretch a little. Oh well, ramen noodles for the next two to three nights it is.

BB's isn't as busy as normal for a Monday morning. I am served quickly and grab my optimal spot to people watch. I know that I made the right decision to attend school in New York as I'd planned with him. Even though I'm here without him.

After mom had abruptly stopped working for the Mulligans, I considered attending college in California instead. This would've been the best option, distancing myself from him.

For the first couple of weeks, I was afraid that I would run into him and wondered how I would've reacted, but the campus is big enough. I am now in my junior year, and I still haven't had the pleasure of coming across him.

Knowing him, he probably stuck to the life his family mapped out for him and attended Harvard.

I gaze out the window and watch as the busy swarm of worker bees bustle up and down the street to their destinations. I often wonder what's going through their minds. I take in their facial expressions, which reveal so much but so little at the same time. Are they thinking about work, kids, finances, or their mistresses?

Can they see the anxiety written on mine?

"Titanium" by Sia blasts through my headphones as I head to my first class. It boosts my mood, and I think there's nothing that could come my way today that I won't be able to conquer.

I have fifteen minutes to spare. This is the only time I have to go over my notes before my macroeconomics test. Professor Smith, also known as "Shark" or "Lucifer" is well known for her difficult quizzes. If I receive a C in this class, it will be a cause for a full-out celebration. If you receive an A, well, you are a fucking genius and should be teaching.

A couple minutes into my studying, I hear the steady vibration of my cellphone. I hesitate, not sure if I should take the call or study. The latter loses. I was hoping my Econ class had been cancelled. Wishful thinking: it's Tinea.

Tinea's birthday is coming up, and she has been driving me up the wall for the past three weeks about the party. I don't know what her wedding is going to be like if she has planned a week-long celebration just for her twenty-first. The main celebration is going to be at the hottest night club in Manhattan, called the Syders, this Saturday.

Next month, the hottest night club in the city will be something else.

"Good morning, Tinea."

"Hey, sunshine! You on your way to class?"

"Yeah, what's up?"

"Quick question … you sure you'll be at Syders Saturday, right?"

Why is she asking? It's not as if I had an option. She would be pissed if I missed the grand finale.

"You are acting like I have a choice. Do I have a choice?"

Clubbing has never been my thing. If she is going to give me an out, I would be more than happy to take it.

"Hell no, Simone! You know better than that."

"So, why are you asking?" A tingling sensation begins crawling up my sleeve. I hate when she does crap like this. I am not going out on any more blind dates. Our taste in men is night and day.

"I'm just checking."

I laugh. "At times, you are like an annoying sister."

Two weeks ago, Tinea set me up with a lovely, sexy guy named Jorge. He had the looks and the body. She never gets the physical wrong; where she turns sideways is the conversation.

The guy couldn't stop talking about himself for the majority of the dinner.

I mean really … Ask me something! The point of a first date is to get to know each other.

What the hell! That is not a good sign.

Looking down at my Michele Deco Diamond

watch, a gift from my mom, I realize I only have two minutes to get to class. I pack my flashcards and briskly walk to class. Professor Clarke doesn't tolerate tardiness. That happened once because I decided to stop at BB's although I was already running late for class. I needed my cup of Joe, especially after the horrible night I had. My nights are always horrible when I dream about him. I can't be late to this class again.

"No, but I get out at 10:45, and then I have a test at 11:00. Just tell me over the phone."

"Can't. This is too important and delicate to be delivered over the phone."

This witch came to this Earth to torment me. She knows that I will agonize over this "important information" all during class. I won't be focused on the lecture; my mind will be wondering ... what can it be? *She found a new boy toy ... that better not be it. I will be pissed.* I hope someone isn't ill. *She would be more emotional and not so damn chirpy.* Did she not get the DJ she wanted to perform at her party? *Why the hell would that be important to me?*

"Well, it will have to be after my Econ class at noon."

"I can't at noon, I have to finalize the party with the party planner."

Really, witch ... really? I guess it's not that important then, is it?

"I can meet with you in between classes. I promise it won't take longer than two minutes. I will meet you in front of the theatre on West 4th street."

"Fine. Meet me in front of Corridor." I hang up and enter the class just as the professor is preparing to close the door.

5

Needless to say, my class is dry. That could be because I did not hear a word Professor Clarke said. I spent the whole time looking down at my notebook, at the swirls, and lines … *Oh, I think I finally drew a pretty good box.* The page lacks any learning material. Jerry, Mr. Studious as he is known, takes a copious amount of notes. I have to meet up with him later in the week.

Grabbing my supplies, I dash out of my finance class, weaving my way through the crowd. I reach the front of Corridor Theatre and begin scanning the area for the fair skinned, red headed witch.

I have ten minutes to hear this "important information" then get to my Econ class straight across the lot.

I spot her cruising up the steps from the parking lot with two cups labelled BB's, looking as if she just got off a runaway.

I am in no way jealous. I love her, I do, but damn she makes me look as if I don't even try to put myself together. I hate standing next to her. The head turner witch that she is, dressed in a white shirt with a tweed Chanel jacket, dark washed jeans, and high heels (most likely Louboutin's).

Tinea gets her love for fashion from her mom. She has worn name brand apparel from middle school. She was always voted best dressed.

"Hey there." *Okay, here we are, spit it out.*

"How was class?" she asks with mischief dancing in her eyes as she hands me a cup of coffee.

Who cares how class was? Get to the point. I gently push her back; she knows that I am not much of a hugger.

"So, what is it?" I feel my temper rising. I really don't have time for games today, especially since I need to score well on this Econ exam. Eyes squinted, head tilted with no smile or warmth insight, I give her my *don't fuck with me look*.

"Oh, are you ready for it?"

"Any. Day. Now. Witch."

She takes a drink of her coffee. "So, I ran into an old friend of yours yesterday and invited said person to my party on Saturday. I wasn't going to tell you at first, but I knew you would be pissed with me if I didn't." She pauses, I guess for dramatic effect. 'Cause she is a dramatic person.

I am beyond exasperated. "Just spit it out, Tinea," I yell. "You have already wasted seven minutes of my day."

Beyoncé's song "Sorry" starts playing.

"Don't answer that," I scream as she reaches for her phone.

"Tinea Knight," she answers. "Mr. Barnes … of course … my pleasure … no problem at all … I will be there in twenty."

"What the hell, Tinea? I don't have time for this crap today. I now have five minutes to get to my class." I start fuming and begin to walk away.

Sometimes I don't know why she does things like this. Everyone is not on her time. *She knows this class has been difficult for me. What the hell is her problem?*

"Ryan Mulligan." She erupts in laughter, already knowing how this information will affect me. "Don't you have a test to get to?"

My feet are cemented to the ground with the name she yelled. *How is that possible? That is not possible? Where? How? When?*

Tinea always knows how to make a dramatic entrance or exit. This one is a gut puncher.

I look back to ask her the questions that have been

7

swirling in my head. She is halfway across the parking lot.

"Tinea," I yell.

She ignores my call.

My stomach tightens as my body begins to quiver, wishing for the comfort of a warm bed.

I break out of my stupor still not able to shake the quiver through my body, and hurry across the quad to take my Econ test.

Shit, I am going fail.

Chapter Two

I sit on the fourth seat, third row from the back of the class. At the beginning of the semester, Econ: Competitive Analysis started off with one hundred students. By day fifteen, there were only seventy-five students left.

I don't recall when Professor Shark entered the class. I look quizzically at a sheet of paper that magically appears on my desk.

What the hell is this?

My mind goes blank. The jumbled words on the paper dance to their own tune.

Snap out of it, Simone.

I can't fail this class. I have a B- and I need to get a B or A-to try and maintain my grade point average.

I close my eyes, shake my head, and look back down on the table. I bend sideways out of my chair to retrieve a pencil from the side pocket of my backpack.

I sit back, take a heavy breath, count to ten, and start the test.

Professor Shark calls time. I walk at a leisurely pace toward my professor, scanning the paper for any errors.

"Ms. Goodman, I don't have all day," snaps a stern voice.

"My apologies, professor." I hand her my paper and briskly exit the room.

I ignore the chimes from my phone, choosing

instead to occupy my mind with the news that Tinea shared with me earlier.

I glance at my watch; it's only 11:50a.m. My movie marketing class is at 1:00 p.m. I normally would go grab something to eat but I have no appetite.

Forget it, I will get the notes from Paul tomorrow.

I make a beeline for the subway, destination: la casa.

I walk into the apartment and up the flight of stairs to the bedroom on the right. I push the backpack off my shoulder, a loud thud echoing in the room. I pull my arms out of my jacket, dropping it on the wooden floor.

I need a Xanax. Jackie.

I jog down the stairs and speed walk down the hallway to Jackie's bathroom. I search through her medicine cabinet.

Where is the bottle? Gotcha. I open the bottle, pop the pill in my mouth and turn on the faucet, washing the pill down my throat.

With my mission accomplished, I walk back to my room, kick off my shoes, and lay on my queen bed. My body slowly drifts into unconsciousness.

Chapter Three

Past

At the age of seventeen, I knew that Ryan Mulligan was the love of my life. No one could have told me different.

How long ago that seems …

At the time, I called West Palm Beach home. Living in the "Sunshine State" didn't mean my life was always sunny. There were some scattered showers and thunderstorms.

I first met Ryan at the age of five. My mom worked as the head housekeeper for the Mulligans' on "The Island" where the wealthy and famous resided.

Ryan and I had a lot of fun together. I was a bit of a tomboy, not afraid to climb or crawl through anything. That all changed during our tween years. Once he turned eleven, I was the last person on his mind. A switch turned on, and our friendship died. At times, he would say hello and give a lingering look, other times silence.

Sophomore year, my mom guilted me into spending two hours each day after school with her at the Mulligans'. I fought back, but my fight was futile. What she didn't understand was that I stopped looking forward to going to the Mulligans' six years ago.

Can you hear it? The guilt trip that parents love to give.

You are going off to college in three years. You are my only daughter. Blah, blah, blah.

So here I am at the glass, oval table in the corner of the kitchen completing homework, while my mom peels sweet potatoes.

Guess someone requested her famous pie.

The smell of citrus and wood hits my nose. It must be his cologne or body wash.

"Hey, Ms. Rose," Ryan state, entering the kitchen. "Simone."

His voice is so stoic whenever he says my name. My eyes briefly move toward the ceiling.

I glance at Ryan as he grabs an apple and a bottle of Fuji water before heading out the door toward the pool. Ryan throws his shirt on the lounge chair.

OMG …

OMG …

He is no longer that eleven-year-old boy.

Damn!

He is a man with a heavenly, sexy body. He has abs—a six pack, to be exact—and a v-line going down into his swim trunks.

His body is stuff I read about. He's wunderland. I like the German way of saying wonderland ever since I read it in a fantasy novel last year. I am definitely adding him to my wunderland list.

Absentmindedly, I wipe water off my hand.

Wait, how did that get there? Oh, crap … Water slides down my chin onto my hand.

I scan the kitchen, ensuring that my mom didn't see the way I was reacting to the gloriousness of Ryan's body.

Trying hard to refocus on the task at hand, I begin admiring the crown moldings white cabinets, the gold knobs, and pulls. Three single jar pendants perfectly hang in the center of the massive, white, marble island, with strategically placed espresso bar stools. I have always admired how immaculately the Mulligans' house is designed. Each piece of furniture, paintings, and fixtures have a purpose.

The rumbling coming from my stomach caused by the aroma of the sweet potato pies reminds me that I hadn't eaten lunch. The tempting pies lay on the counter waiting to be devoured.

"Rose, my love, is one of those pies for me?"

Smiling from ear to ear, my mom replies, "One slice, Ryan, one."

"Thanks," he replies with a kiss on her cheek.

He halts as he exits the kitchen with a grin the size of Texas. "Hey, Simone."

I shudder. "Hhhhiiii … hey." I am bemused at his greeting. He doesn't seem as distant today.

Laughing, he continues on his way.

Mom gives me a scowl. She stares at me as if she's able to read all my not-so-good thoughts going through my head about Ryan. I become uncomfortable under her gaze. Thinking of a way to distract her, I offer her a helping hand and prepare the pie for him.

"Can you take the pie up to Ryan, sweetie? I forgot about something I need to have done before Mrs. Mulligan gets back."

After asking, she hesitates as if she isn't sure she should ask this of me.

Excitement and trepidation hit me all at once. It's been years since I was allowed to enter Ryan's room.

"I can do that." My hand shakes as I pick up the pie.

The wood creaks as I hold onto the banister. *Mom would be pissed if the plate broke; I would be mortified.*

Five more steps to Ryan's door. I hold on to the

13

plate with both hands as they begin to tremble. *Inhale. Exhale.* The sound of a beating drum grows louder and louder the closer I got to his door. *Get it together, Simone. You're just delivering pie.*

Listening to the rock music blasting from his room, I hesitate to knock.

What will his reaction be when he sees it's me instead of my mom? Will he be aloof? There is only one way to find out.

I bang on the door loud enough to be heard over the blaring music.

"Come in."

Inhale, exhale.

Scouring his room, it's nothing like I have imagined. Something seems to be missing. *What is it?*

The room is as big as my entire apartment. The blue walls and brown furnishing exude masculinity—a brown, tufted, leather couch and tall, four-poster bed. The only item mounted on the wall is a sixty-five-inch TV.

Aaahhh ... that's it. There's no clothing laying on the floor. I would think that a boy's room would be messy; clothing, paper everywhere. I know that I'm stereotyping, but that's the word on the street. Guess Mom ensures his room is cleaned daily.

"Simone." I jump at the surprise in his voice, finding a huge grin on his face.

I stop and begin to examine him, taking in all the features of my old friend. He has grown into a handsome man. *He must drive the girls at Queens Academy crazy.* Ryan looks to be over six feet tall with an athletic built. Mom said that he is part of the lacrosse and swim team at his school. If he is not in his room or out with friends, you could find him in the gym in the basement. His brown hair is cut short on the sides, long enough

14

up top to be spiked. His green eyes spark with dashes of gold flecks as he smiles with deep dimples that makes me melt. He stands with such sexy confidence.

God has surely created some amazing creatures on this Earth. His eyes gaze upon my lips, as I lick them.

Laughing he asks, "Is this for me?"

"Oh, yeah. Here's your pie. Where would you like me to put it?"

"I can take it."

Handing off the pie, I head for the exit. The faster I get out of here, the faster the chest palpitations will stop.

"Where are you rushing off to?"

"Just to help Mom. Did you need anything else?" I ask, taking this moment to get one last look at him.

"Quick question: What grade are you in again?"

"I'm a junior. Why?"

"Just needed help with this calculus problem. I overheard your mom bragging to Dad about you taking advanced calculus."

So embarrassing, Mom bragging about me like this. It's not like I won a beauty contest or something. It's just advanced calculus. My body feels heated, so I know my cheeks look like a red apple.

"Actually, numbers are the one thing I feel I do comprehend."

"Great, let me get my book. I can't afford to fail this class."

I watch as he walks over to his desk and grabs his book, then turns and sits on the couch. *What is he doing?*

"Are you going to tutor me from over there, or are you going to sit?" he asks with amusement dancing in his eyes.

What the hell is he talking about? "I didn't agree to tutor

15

you. You asked a simple question; how did my answer get construed into me tutoring you?" *What the hell is wrong with this boy? You may be hot, but I don't work for you.*

He slants his head as he knits his brows, squinting and staring at me as if I am a conundrum. He shakes his head and smiles.

"You tutoring me. I thought that was obvious."

Obnoxious, isn't he? Just because my mother works for his family doesn't mean I work for him.

"No! It wasn't obvious to me. You can ask me nicely, then it's still up to me to say yes or no." I place my hands on my hips and give him my *come at me* look.

He holds up his hands as he rises from the sofa. "I'm sorry, firecracker. You're here every afternoon, so I just figured instead of helping your mom you could spend time helping me."

He stops in front of me and drops down to his knees. His hands clasp together as if he is about to pray to the heavens above.

"Simone, could you please, please help me? I will be forever grateful." Those lovely, green orbs sparkle.

Err ... what do I say? I should ask Mom first, see if it's a good idea? Let him sweat. *Girl, you know you want to say yes; look at this hot man on his knees in front of you.* "Let me think about it."

He stands way too close for my liking. I can smell his woodsy scent. His height is intimidating but perfect, his lips, smile, eyes, and body are playing with my senses. He knows he is good-looking, and he is not afraid to use his charms as a weapon. Woo ... he plays dirty, and I like it.

Snap out of it, Simone, and back away. I begin stepping backward toward the door. Each step I take, he advances until I am trapped between his body and the door.

"What do you have to think about? You are here every afternoon anyway."

"And? Couldn't it be possible that I could find a better use of my time?"

He smirks and licks his lips. "No."

My chest rises and falls in rapid succession. I don't know if it's from anger. I can feel the heat permeating from his body and something I cannot describe in the green orbits of his eyes. My breasts feel weird. *Why are my nipples hardening?* A weird sensation is coursing through my body. *This is ridiculous. What is happening to me?* I bite my lip, thinking it would help me get control of my wayward thoughts and feeling. No such luck.

"Can you please excuse me, Mr. Mulligan?" The voice sounds foreign to my ears.

"You're beautiful."

What! *Where the hell is this coming from?* He just said I am beautiful. My heart rate doubles. *I can't believe Ryan thinks I'm beautiful.* This hot specimen of a man thinks that I am beautiful.

I stretch my trembling hands behind me, trying to reach the doorknob, with no success. The sooner I get out of this situation, the better. I have to talk with Tinea about this and try to get a hold of the stimulations in my body.

"So, are you?" *Really … really … Simone, that's your reply.* "I have to get back downstairs; Mom must be wondering what's taking so long."

"Answer the question first."

"Fine. We can start tomorrow."

"Can't wait."

He backs away, and I am shocked that I miss the close proximity. Placing his hand on my hip, Ryan opens the door. Walking briskly down the stairs, I

17

begin thinking about Mom and the twenty questions she is going to ask upon my return. Dropping off pie surely took longer than it should.

"Thank you!" he yells.

I turn around as I hit the bottom step and shout my reply. "You're welcome."

"Sorry it took me so long," I state upon entering the kitchen. I see that look on my mother's face. I never like the accusation stare. I actually like to be guilty of my deeds whenever she gives me that look. At least then I know I earned it.

"It took a long time just to drop off a slice a pie."

I sit at the kitchen island and relay what transpired with Ryan. Of course, I deleted most of the conversation. Especially him calling me beautiful.

"Well, I hope you said yes."

"I did."

"Thank you, baby. Now, did you get all your homework finished?"

"No, ma'am." I go back to my corner and try to resume my work. After ten minutes, I realize it's a lost cause. My mind keeps drifting back to Ryan. Analyzing his room, his every facial expression, body, and actions that took place between us.

Chapter Four

The past couple weeks have been interesting, to say the least. Tutoring Ryan hasn't been as bad as I thought it would be. He caught on pretty quickly, which made it easier for us to cover a lot of information in three weeks. It's also been nice getting to know the man that my old friend has grown up to be. He isn't the entitled, obnoxious ass I thought he was. He is charismatic, funny, caring, and actually listens when I speak.

Ryan also adores and respects my mom dearly; for that, my heart quivers for him more. My mom has known him since he was five. They bonded in a way only a mother could. I have overheard him introducing her to his friends as his second mom. He seeks advice from her before his own parents.

His mother, Christina, spends her time playing tennis, lunching, shopping, throwing dinner parties; to sum that all up into one word: "socializing." Well, I should back up. I have to give her credit for all the good philanthropic work she does. Education has been one of her biggest focuses, especially for kids.

While his dad, Robert, spends his time building exquisite architecture. He has offices in New York, London, Paris, and California, with his main office in downtown West Palm Beach. His most recent building is the exquisite, thirty-three story condominium Astoria Towers in New York. You can't even see the inside of the building before providing financials to ensure that you can afford it.

After a quick snack, I begin peeling carrots and potatoes for the stew that mom is making for the Mulligans' dinner. While sitting on pins and needles waiting to see if all the tutoring sessions have been worth it. Ryan took his mid-term math test yesterday and would be getting his results today.

An image of Mrs. Mulligan's face pops in my head the day she found us in Ryan's room.

"What's going on in here?"

Startled, I turned to find the owner of the accusing tone at the door way. Ever the dresser, Mrs. Mulligan stands in the door way looking nothing less than perfection. Dressed in a sharp, navy, wide leg pants suit, her golden blonde hair is in a bun with not a strand out of place. Her makeup looks effortless and natural.

She squints and surveys the room, bringing her eyes back to us on Ryan's bed.

"I'm waiting for an answer."

Ryan sighs and replies, "Studying, Mom," his hands gesture to the books, paper, and calculator on the bed.

"Would the bedroom be an appropriate place for studying? I know for a fact that we have a lovely office with chairs downstairs. Son, utilize it."

Frozen, I cannot take my eyes off Mrs. Mulligan. I know this is not a good look, but we weren't doing anything wrong. Yes, we could have chosen a different area in his room to study; there is a couch, desk, gosh even the area rug. I didn't pick the bed. He was already on it. I sat down on the opposite side, eventually I got comfortable, and that's that.

"Fine, will do in the future," he crassly replies.

"Now, Ryan."

A chill courses through me as Mrs. Mulligan says those words. I come out of my stupor, hop off the bed, grab my stuff,

and hastily exit the room. I don't remember how I got to the
library downstairs, but I got there.

Never wanting to experience that again, the library became
our place of study.

"You're the best." Ryan states in my left ear.

"Aahh."

Lost in my memories, I didn't hear or see when Ryan entered the kitchen. The knife runs across my index finger as it falls onto the floor.

"Oh shit, I'm sorry, Simone," Ryan says. "Hell, you're bleeding."

"I'll be okay."

Mom rushes into the kitchen. "What's wrong?"

"Nothing."

"You're bleeding, Simone."

"I will be fine, it's just a little cut on my index finger."

Moving to the kitchen faucet, I turn on the water, making sure it's cold before placing my finger under the running water. It sooths the stinging sensation and helps the bleeding to subside.

"I will grab the first aid kit," Ryan says as he exits the kitchen.

Mom takes my finger and begins applying pressure with a paper towel. *You would think the wound is fatal. It's like a paper cut, for crying out loud. How many people get those per year? I'm not gushing blood.*

Taking a deep breath, I reiterate that I'm just fine and the cut isn't that bad. Shaking my head, I look to the heavens.

"I got it," Ryan says, taking a seat at the kitchen counter. "Let me see."

I can see the concern in his eyes.

"I'm good. See?" I hold up the finger to show that

there is hardly any blood dripping.

"Come here, let me see it," he firmly states.

This sounds more like a command instead of a request. Squinting, I look into his hard, green orbs. *You don't command me.* Trying to be strong, I find myself moving across to the counter.

I rest against the chair as he takes my finger, shaking his head as he inspects the slash. Ryan gently cleans the wound with an alcohol antiseptic pad, rubs on antibiotic cream, and seals it with a band aid.

"Better," he says with relief.

"Better." I nod. I can tell he's doing this because he feels the accident was his fault. I guess it isn't bad to have a smoking hot ass worry about me, even if is a little too much.

Flexing my finger, I wink at him, and those dimples make an appearance.

"It feels better," I say again for confirmation as I head back for the bowl of vegetables that I was peeling before this mini drama happened.

"Simone, leaves those be, and just relax," says my mom.

"Mom, the finger is okay. I can help you."

"Do as I say, young lady."

I can hear the sternness in her voice. That's definitely not a request, but a command.

Holding my hands up, I back away from the bowl. "Fine." Looking around, I find Ryan sitting at the breakfast table and venture over to see about getting our tutoring session started.

"So, Ryan, how was your day today? Anything exciting or more entertaining than what happened to me earlier?"

"No, not much, but thanks to you I did get a 95 on

my mid-term," he says beaming from ear-to-ear.

"Really now," I say, popping my collar. "I guess I am the best." An ecstatic feeling overtakes my body. I'm overjoyed that I was able to help him accomplish this.

"I guess you are," he laughs.

"Okay, well, you still are not a genius, so let's get going."

"Since you got injured and all, you can take the day off. Relax, and we will pick it up again tomorrow."

"Oh … how gracious of you, Mr. Mulligan," I say, laughing. "Well, since I am not needed by anyone today, I believe I will go enjoy a book by the pool." Waving goodbye to Ryan and Mom, I head toward the patio door. The sun is shining, and the pool is glistening. This is exactly what the doctor ordered. I shiver as I feel him watching me. I put a little more swing in my step, knowing he's enjoying the view.

Chapter Five

Two weeks have passed since the knife catastrophe. Mom is working late tonight; the Mulligans are having a dinner party. The cleaning service dusted, mopped, and polished every corner and crevice of this house—not a speck of dust can be found. They hired a top-notch catering service.

Glancing at the fancy menu, I see that it includes escargot and caviar.

I gag on the ham sandwich I'm consuming. *Who eats this crap? There is no way this crap tastes good.*

Hmmm … I would eat this sweet potato pie that Mom made though. I hope she made one for our house.

"Rose, everything looks lovely," Mrs. Mulligan states as she enters into the kitchen. "Do you think we have enough food?"

"You should be good, ma'am," mom replies.

Staring at my mom, her eyes looked sluggish. Mrs. Mulligan's dinner parties are a two-week preparation event. Although my mom hires additional cleaners, chefs, and florists, she has to ensure that all the tasks are executed effortlessly. It's all on her shoulder, and it takes a lot out of her. Once the planning begins, Mrs. Mulligan makes numerous changes before settling on a concept she finds exceptional. The floral arrangement is a task … one day she wants pink peonies, and the next day it's white hydrangeas or maybe a mixture of both.

Mom always seems drained during any of these elaborate parties or dinners. When it comes time for Mrs. Mulligans' philanthropic events, I stay out of my mom's way. She becomes a woman I don't recognize. Her mood becomes colorful.

"The Perkins will be in attendance tonight, and they are bringing their lovely daughter, Madeline," she says with glee in her eyes. She turns, looking at me with a smirk.

Ha. That statement was made for me.

"That will be nice. Ryan will have someone to converse with," my mom says as she continues placing the plate settings on the table.

"I think Ryan will actually enjoy himself this time. He tried to get out of attending, but I twisted his arm." She winks and laughs. "As always, everything looks great, Rose. I don't know what I would do without you."

"Thanks," Mom replies to Mrs. Mulligan's retreating form.

She is such a … I can't find the right word.
Bitch.
That's the word. Bitch.

I watch as Mrs. Mulligan strolls up the stairs to her batch of professionals waiting to ensure that she looks gorgeous tonight.

I know that she brought up Madeline because of me. The weirdest sensation shook me the moment when she mentioned her. I can't pinpoint the emotion. Is it jealousy? I have nothing to feel jealous about. I am not Ryan's girlfriend in any way. It's nice daydreaming that we were more, but I know that will never happen.

Still, I don't think I like this feeling.

I leave my mom and head to the kitchen breakfast

bar and begin working on my homework, getting some of it out the way for the weekend.

"Sim, what are you still doing here?" Ryan asks, entering the kitchen, looking like he is about to do a photoshoot for the cover of GQ or Vogue. A teenager should not look this good.

Good God Almighty!

"Just waiting for Uncle Sam. Mom is going to be here for a while tonight ensuring this show runs properly."

"Yep, can't wait for this to be over with."

"Hey, baby girl," my uncle calls as he comes into the room. "Ready to go?"

"Yeah, give me a minute." I begin packing my history book and supplies into my backpack. Looking up from packing, Ryan's eyes are sad and his demeanor seems desolate.

Smiling, I give him a hug. "Have fun tonight."

"Eh."

I erupt in laughter as I leave with Uncle Sam.

That night as I lay in my bed, my mind wonders about the dinner party. I don't care if the Mulligans' guests enjoyed the food or decor. I wonder if Ryan is having a good time with Madeline. What they were talking about ... Does he like her as a friend or is there more? Does she look beautiful in her dress?

Of course, she does. I can say that the few times I have had the honor to meet her ... well, let's just say it wasn't an honor. The look of disgust and disinterest that she gave me when Ryan introduced me to her couple years ago, told me everything I needed to know about her.

She is an uppity snob who thinks that she can treat people rudely because her family has wealth.

I place my right hand beneath my pillow and sigh as I recall the way Ryan was dressed. Gray dress slacks, black dress shirt rolled up to the elbows, with black loafers.

Hmm...

Hugging him didn't help either. I felt myself shiver when I smelled his cologne. That smell. The scent of cedar, apple, lemon, and there was something else but I can't put my finger on it.

"These Are the Times" starts by Dru Hill. Shaking my head, I turn sideways and snatch my phone from the side table. I know it's my best friend, Tinea, calling.

Tinea always called me with some gossip. She is the Enquirer, Us Weekly, People, and Ok Magazine all rolled into one. If there was anything happening or was about to happen, she knew about it. I don't know how she did it, but she was good. Of course, she wants to either be a journalist or a lawyer. She will be successful doing either.

"Hey."

"Hey, what are you up to?" the voice asks.

This is not a girl's voice, definitely not Tinea. This voice reminds me of hot chocolate.

I quickly look at the phone and don't recognize the phone number. I don't have many friends, so who the hell could this be?

"Who is this?"

"Who were you expecting?"

"Who is this?" I ask with a snap in my voice. "If you

don't tell me who you are, I am going to hang up."

Laughter comes from the other end of the phone. "It's Ryan, Sim. So snappy. Who were you expecting? Hope it wasn't some other dude."

"Ryan?" I say quizzically as my heart begins to race. He has never called me before. He doesn't even have my number. "How did you get my phone number?"

"I have my ways. You didn't answer my question … who were you expecting?"

"Mom gave you the number most likely," I reply, laughing. "I was expecting Tinea. Why are you calling me?"

"I am utterly bored. I had to lie my way out of the rest of dinner."

He probably lied and said his stomach hurt or something stupid. It's Ryan, so it had to be more creative than that, I think, shaking my head with a colossal grin on my face.

The guy that I was just night dreaming about called me.

Me.

"Not enjoying your companionship?"

"She bored me stiff. She just kept talking about herself and stupid crap that I care nothing about. I would rather spend my time with you."

Pause.

I stopped breathing.

What?

"Wow! Are you flirting with me, Ryan?" I giggle.

I slap my forehead. *Giggled. You giggled.* It was not even a good, flirty giggle. Oh gosh, I need help.

"Isn't it obvious? I have been flirting with you for the past couple weeks, Sim. You keep brushing me off."

What?

What?

When?

I am smiling so hard my face hurts. I place the phone down on the bed and scream into my fist. I take a couple seconds to collect myself and resume the call.

"Since you pointed it out. No, not really. Maybe I need to pay better attention."

"Or I need to do a better job," he replies.

Damn it, did I just pee myself!?

Chapter Six

We talked on the phone for hours last night. Throughout the past couple weeks, I can see that we had begun getting back the friendship that had fizzled years ago.

The first few weeks of tutoring, our conversation mainly consisted of "hi" or "how was your day?" I was awkward and nervous while he remained self-assured and hot.

My mom would give us a snack and then we would head to library, since we were banned from using Ryan's bedroom.

As weeks went on, I became myself around him. I wasn't afraid to make jokes even if they weren't that funny, ruffle his hair like I did when we were younger, or punch him.

After our conversation last night, I could see where, at times, he had become flirty. The way the tenor of his voice changed when he told me that I looked beautiful. Or the times I caught him staring at me with a puzzled look.

Those puzzled looks left me feeling self-conscious, examining myself from head to toe to see if my clothing was out of place; sneakily pulling up my camera app on my phone to ensure that there wasn't any food in my teeth or if my hair was crazy.

Last night, we spoke about everything and anything. I learned about his favorite movie, which I always thought was X-Men, but I guess that was when we were younger. He no longer loved blue, but brown; not just any brown, but hazel brown.

I found that suspicious since that was the colors of my eyes. I may have swooned a little, just a little.

His favorite day of the week is Saturday. Saturday mornings, he and his dad spend time together golfing or fishing. Men bonding time. If his dad had to travel out of state, which he did often, he tried to ensure that he was back by Friday.

He's looking forward to college, finally being able to be on his own. His father's and grandfather's Alma Mater is Harvard but that's not his first choice. Ryan really wants to attend NYU. He did try to broach that subject with his folks, but they ignored him.

Mr. Mulligan owns one of the biggest architectural and developmental firms in the country. The Mulligans Group has offices in New York, California, Florida, London, Paris and recently opened a satellite office in Arizona. Ryan is expected to be president and CEO one day.

Ryan looks forward to the day that he can walk by a building and know that he had a hand in its construction. He speaks of architecture with such passion.

I know without a doubt that he was born for this.

"One day, if you are on your best behavior, I will let you see my sketch pad," he teased.

"I will try."

We spoke about my aspiration and dreams of working in the advertising industry. We joked about all the ridiculous ads on television and discussed how I would have done it.

Time flew. I didn't realize that we had been on the

phone for hours until my mom got home a little after midnight.

I didn't want our conversation to end, but I didn't want my mom to catch me on the phone with him. I decided it was best to end the conversation.

I lay awake for another two hours replaying the phone conversation with Ryan in a loop.

I think about my life, at times wishing that my mom was rich or that my dad would be an active parent in my life. Realization hits me like a ton of bricks; life isn't always better on the other side.

Yeah, he drives a Porsche, goes to the best private school, wears designer labels, lives in a house on the Atlantic Ocean, and so many other things.

Ryan's parents are rich, he can have all that he desires, but it comes with restrictions and limitations. Not having free will of your journey through life.

Wow…

Chapter Seven

Tutoring sessions have dwindled to only two hours on Saturdays, while our phone calls and texting become a nightly routine. We talk to each other for hours once Ryan gets through with Lacrosse practice.

We've finally gotten back to the place where we left off years ago. I feel that I can talk with him about pretty much anything.

Dreaming and wishing for more than a friendship.

Junior prom is within two weeks. I have been asked by three guys, which was all unexpected. I still haven't made a decision.

Andrew Dean, Brian Simpson, and Marc Tall. All three men have qualities that I like. The jock, bad boy, and nerd, which they could all be rolled into one.

Tinea thinks that it's stupid that I didn't jump at the chance to accept Brian Simpson's offer. After all, he is the captain of the football team and student body president.

He is tall, with brown eyes, wears his hair in a low fade, and is smooth like a dark Cadbury chocolate bar.

Unfortunately, he still doesn't compare to Ry. Yeah, I said Ry, that's what I call Ryan now.

Although deep within me I would love for Ryan to escort me to my prom, I know that it's only a fantasy. Reality is Brian asked and is willing.

The bowl of warm, brandy wined apples and vanilla ice cream is a welcome treat on this rainy, Monday afternoon. I'm lost in the motion of Ryan's actions as he swirls his tongue around his spoon filled with the delicious dessert. My spoon clatters to the floor.

"Crap." I jump up, cleaning the mess off the kitchen floor as Ryan erupts in laughter.

I gather a few wet paper towels and wipe the area where the spoon fell again, ensuring there's no trace of stickiness from the cream.

"Simone, the prom is next weekend, right?" my mom asks.

I freeze. Why is she bringing this up now?

"Yeah, Mom." I move toward the trash bin, disposing of the tissues. "I will be going shopping with Tinea tomorrow, so I won't be coming by after school," I mention as I finish washing out my bowl.

"Who are you going with?"

Why, why, why is she asking me this right at this present moment? I can feel his eyes drilling into my back. Placing my bowl in the dishwasher, I brace against the counter and wait for the onslaught of questions I know are coming.

"Brian Simpson."

The sound of the kitchenette chair grabs my attention. I'm not expecting to see the vision in front of me.

Ryan eyes are cold as ice. Anger radiates from him.

"Oh. Brian Simpson the boyfriend?"

"No," I reply with a hint of confusion and unease.

"He's the captain of the football team. He asked, and I said yes. Besides, how do you tell the captain of the football team no?" I shrug, moving slowly across the room toward my book bag.

"Very easily," he states dryly. "No!"

I grab my book bag and glare at Ryan across the table, licking my lips. I'm not quite sure what my response should be.

My mom in the corner pretending that she is not seeing what's happening. Me, thinking I am in a different hemisphere. I can't comprehend why he is acting this way.

Was I being naive?

"Since we are both here, why don't you meet me in the library so we can get some work done?" he says as he leaves the kitchen.

What the hell is his problem?

We were just sitting here eye fucking each other. Enjoying our apples, then mom just had to bring up prom. I hadn't mentioned it to Ryan. Why should I?

Could he be jealous? No. I shook my head at that fleeting thought.

"Mom, I will see you in a bit."

The Mulligans' home library is a dream. This library is one of my must haves in life.

Upon entering the library, the first thing that catches my eyes is the ocean. Nothing but miles upon miles of the ocean. That's made possible by the endless exterior wall built with translucent glass.

The glass helps to create different shades of light from a mixture of blues and violets at sunrise to hues of yellow, orange, and reds at sunset. Although sunrise and sunsets are beautiful, it cannot compare to night time. Just sitting watching the twinkling stars while the moon cascades off the ocean floor.

That view—is magical.

To the right and left of the room, floor to ceiling shelves lines the inner walls with a ladder sitting to the right of each wall.

The center of the room is made of different sized chairs, sofas, and chaises organized in such a way that no matter where you sit, you have a view of outside.

There are no desks in this room. It's solely meant for relaxation and reading.

Can you say heaven …?

Ryan rises from the white sofa and walks swiftly to me. His six-two frame towers above me. Lookingdown at me, he sighs

"I don't want you to go to the prom with that guy."

"Excuse me?"

"Don't go to the prom."

What? Is he serious? Slanting my head, akimbo, I look at him in confusion.

"Why would I do that?"

"Simone, just don't go." He runs his hand down his face.

Throwing my hands up, I reply. "I want to go. I have to attend. I want to attend. I am going!"

He can't tell me what to do. I am not his girlfriend, nor do I work for him. My mother is the only person fully authorized to dictate my life.

Grabbing his hair, he begins mumbling incoherent words. He turns and begins walking back towards the coach, abruptly stopping. Within an instant, we stand chest to nose, unleashing havoc on my senses.

Shivers run through my body. I gulp down my spit, hesitantly looking at him under my lashes.

He slips his hands on my cheeks, questions in his eyes. Leaning forward, he kisses me.

It's slow, sweet, slow, everything I read about and never knew I wanted in a first kiss. Hermann Hesse described this moment the best: "I felt something melt inside of me, that hurt in an exquisite way. All the secrets that slept deep within me came awake. Everything was transformed and enchanted, everything made sense."

As the kiss grew, my mouth opens and our tongues intertwine. Time stands still. I don't want this euphoria to end.

He slowly pulls my bottom lip between his teeth, releasing my lip with a lazy tug. Ryan looks into my eyes with longing.

Biting my lip, he leans back in with a simple peck.

OMG! I just had my first kiss. Smiling, I touch my lip.

Taking my hand in his, Ryan leads me to the oblong sofa he abandoned upon my entry. He sensually rubs up and down my forearm. Warmth envelops me as we sit here in silence, ogling each other.

"You don't know how long I have been dying to do that," Ryan says, breaking the silence.

"How long?"

"Way too long."

"You should do it again."

Laughter rings before he kisses me again.

"You really want to attend prom?"

"Yes."

"Fine. I will take you, not that dude," he says with finality.

Someone please pinch me. I must be dreaming. First, Ryan kissed me. Something that he has been dying to do. Now he is going to take me to prom. This day is turning out to be the best day of my life.

Wait, I already told Brian I would be attending prom with him. How can I change my mind now? Prom is within two weeks. And what will Ryan's parents say about him escorting me to prom? I don't know if his mom would be pleased.

"What's that look?"

"Are you going to tell your parents that you're going to take me to prom?"

"Honestly, no," he replies sheepishly. "I want to be with you. I don't just want a friendship with you, I want to be *with* you. Look there are … a few things in my life that I would like to keep private. I want us to see where this will go before we tell people. If you want tobe with me too, then we would need to keep this fromthem."

"Why would you want to keep it private? Am I not as good as Madeline?"

"What! Don't be ridiculous. I am not here kissing and asking to be with Madeline, am I?" Ryan runs his hand down his face in exasperation.

"I guess not."

"You are much prettier, sexier, and smarter than Madeline. You don't need to worry about her."

"Okay. I will keep it between us."

"Great," he exhales.

"There's still the concern of Brian. I feel terrible. How do I tell Brian that I can't go to prom with him anymore, then show up with another guy?"

"You are a sweet person, but I think that you should just be honest. Let him know that you are going with your boyfriend."

Chapter Eight

"Will you stop fidgeting?" Tinea scolds as she drives us to the mall.

"I don't know how I am going to do this," I reply, tapping my feet against the floorboard.

It's been a strenuous day, ditching into classrooms, bathrooms, the library. All trying to avoid coming into contact with Brian.

I woke up feeling strong and that I could conquer the day. I would be able to have a civilized conversation with Brian about backing out of prom. I could do that.

That lasted until I entered school and spotted him standing at his locker talking with his crew. To make matters worse, he could sense me looking at him. He looked up and smiled at me.

I panicked. My feet moved without me thinking it. I ran into the bathroom.

There is no way I will be able to tell him this today. Tomorrow would be better.

"What's up with you? You've been acting weird all day today."

"I have to let Brian know that I can't attend prom with him."

Tinea gawks at me in shock.

"Why not? Are you stupid?"

I bury my face into my hands. "Ryan wants to take me instead," I say through my fingers.

"Ryan who?" Tinea asks, tugging my hands away

from my face. "We don't know a Ryan."

"You don't. I do."

"Wait!"

She swings the Mercedes into a parking spot outside the entrance of L'Estelle, the fancy dress store we decided to shop at for our prom dress.

"The guy that you are tutoring? The Ryan Mulligan guy? The one you argued with me adamantly that you didn't like? The one I told you, you liked? That Ryan?"

Tinea's arms move faster than the words coming out of her mouth. I duck, knowing that her next move would be to smack my arm.

"Ouch."

I nod. "Yeah, that Ryan. I am going to tell you something, don't freak out. Don't smack my arm again either," I say, pointing my index finger.

She sits there silently, waiting, rubbing her hands together.

"Ryan and I kissed yesterday. It was good." I sigh.

I cover my ears from the siren going off in the car.

"Holy hell, Simone, you're blushing," she yells and begins screaming again.

Holy hell, she is loud. I am going to become deaf. During times like these, I normally take a couple steps back, or if we are on the phone I hold the phone away from my ear.

I am sitting in this car, there is nowhere to escape to.

"Wait, a damn minute. He's your first kiss."

I nod and join in on the screaming fest as we both bounce up and down in our seats.

"Now you see my dilemma. How am I going to tell Brian?"

"This is going to be a tricky one. You have to tell

him soon, like tomorrow."

"Yeah, I must do it tomorrow."

I know Ryan is going to ask me about it later. I don't want to start off our relationship with a lie.

"We'll figure it out. I can't believe you waited so long to tell me, witch."

"Sorry. I was just trying to wrap my head around the kiss and all."

"I want to hear everything. Let's get these dresses and head back to my place," she says.

The shopping trip was consummated with two gorgeous dresses. We spend the rest of the afternoon discussing how to approach Brian the following day, and I also give her some details about my first kiss.

"Wow … that kiss must have been good. You had him stunned. He claimed you immediately. My girl got skills," she says as she tumbles back on her bed.

"Shut it …"

"If I was into women, I would test those lips. You would have me proposing." She puckers her lips and simulates us kissing.

I twist my wrist back and forth toward my mouth hoping that she will get the message.

Grabbing a bag of BBQ chips from Tinea's computer desk, we begin studying for tomorrow's science test.

I figured it was best to talk with Brian during our lunch break. "Informing Brian after school would be the best choice; he would able to go to basketball practice and take the frustration out on the court, or he could go home and not have to worry about seeing you for the rest of the day," Tinea pointed out yesterday.

Although those points are all valid, I want to just get it over with.

A hollowness settles in my chest. I never want to be the one to cause someone to be humiliated. I would feel humiliated if the shoe was on the other foot.

Tinea always teased me about Brian having a crush on me. I never believed her. He was always cordial to me, saying hello whenever we passed each other in the halls. We had a few classes together over the years. A few times we partnered on group projects. Although he's a jock, he's very smart.

I never get butterflies when I'm around him. He doesn't make my breathing shallow with just a mere sight of him.

I am so conflicted. I don't comprehend why he would even ask me in the first place. I'm not popular, head of the student council, or head cheerleader. I am by no means referred to as a nerd, although I consistently maintain a 4.0 GPA. I am a normal student at Royal Palm High, not in with the popular crowd nor outcasted.

I wear my hair in a simple high ponytail. Heavy makeup is never my thing—just mascara and lip gloss. I'm a lover of t-shirts and jeans.

I walk leisurely from my third period AP math class headed for the cafeteria. Royal Palm High's overcrowded, noisy cafeteria sits adjacent to the field and the outside palm court. It takes three minutes from math class to reach the cafeteria.

I arrive at the cafeteria with trepidation in my heart. I quickly sift through the crowd in search for Brian. I spot him leaning against the wall surrounded by Suzen and her cohorts.

I avoid these girls like the plague. Shaking my shoulders, I repeat to myself that I would be able to dump my prom date. I briskly walk over, interrupting their conversation.

"Hey, Brian, can I talk with you in private?"

"Rude much, don't you see us talking?" Suzen growls.

Ignoring her, I turn to Brian, pleading with my eyes.
"Sure."

Taking my small hands into his, we exit the cafeteria toward the courtyard. The partly cloudy skies cause a slight chill in the air. The wind makes the palm trees dance.

Extracting my hand, I wrap my arms around my waist.

Brian scouts out an area for us to sit; all the benches are occupied in the courtyard, so we travel to the only empty spot we could find, the outside bleachers.

Why am I doing this? I should do the right thing. Ryan would understand; prom is next week. It isn't right to do this, especially so close to the date. What if Ryan broke up with me over this?

My palms begin to sweat, my feet are jittering. I am a total mess. I have to just get this over with.

"About prom," I say, staring out at the green football field. I am such a coward; I can't even bring myself to look him in the eyes.

"What about prom?" he asks skeptically.

The answer gets stuck in my throat.

"Cat got your tongue? Just say it." He laughs nervously.

"I cannot attend the prom with you. I am so, so, so

44

sorry," I state, placing my sweaty hands tightly together.

"What do you mean you cannot go with me? Are you no longer going?"

Peeking up at him, his face shows how hurt and confused he is.

"No, I am going to the prom, but with someone else," I reply, water leaking out the corners of my eyes.

"You are telling me this now, Simone?" he yells. "Is this a game? Make the football jock look stupid?"

"Of course not," I cry. "I am not that type of person."

"What type of person are you then? 'Cause to me, right now you look like a conniving bitch."

I gasp. The river of tears mingles with the snot running down my face. "I am truly sorry."

"Keep your apology," he says, storming down the bleachers.

Chapter Nine

I can't recall the last time I cried this hard. I hated making an impact on Brian in such a way. It was cruel what I did. I shouldn't have told him during lunch. Tinea was right, I should have waited until the end of the day.

I struggle to pay attention in my other two classes. My mind keeps replaying the conversation I had with Brian and how angry he became.

Can I blame him for being angry?

What else could I have said?

Relief comes to me in the form of the final bell of the day ringing. I quickly grab my books, shoving them inside my backpack. I avoid my locker, eliminating any possibilities of running into Brian. With my head down, I begin my trek to the parking lot to meet Tinea.

My escape is suddenly halted by the skinny, red-headed cheerleader. I'm only ten feet away from the exit. I turn to my right to escape and am blocked in by one of her followers.

I slowly looked up and glare into Suzen's smug face.

Suzen Payne, the head bitch in charge, is the head cheerleader and would make your life a living hell if you crossed her. I try my best to avoid her at all costs.

We have had some minor run ins. She has made snide remarks to me in the past. Depending on the day, I may reply, but most times I hold my head high and ignore her.

I remember one incident in particular. I was at my locker getting my Spanish book for my third period class.

"Hey, *chica*," Ralph said, leaning his right shoulder on the locker to my right.

I smiled. I like Ralph, he clowns around a lot, but he is not clueless.

"Hey, what's up?"

"You ready for Mr. Snows? You know there's a surprise quiz?" he asked as he raised two fingers on both hands, drawing quotation marks in the air. He shook his head and sighed.

I laughed. "Surprise quiz." I leaned my head against the closed locker. "Hopefully there isn't one. It's the first week, for crying out loud."

"Oh goodness, there's a peculiar stench in this area. Right around here," Suzen scoffed, moving her hand in circular motion as she stood across from me.

"It's horrid," Bridgette said as she grabbed her nose holding it with her left hand.

"Simone, did you wash your clothes before wearing them?" Suzen asked, her voice becoming louder and louder. "I mean, I know you wore that shirt all last year. The least you could do is wash it if you can't afford to buy a new one. You know cleanliness is next to godliness."

Laughter rang out in the hall from the all the students that had stopped in the hall to view the Suzen show.

I turned and looked at Ralph, who stood there with his brow knitted and his jaw clenched. His eyes were saying, "Are you going to handle this bitch or should I."

I closed my eyes, dragging breath in and out of my

47

body. I turned around to face Suzen, looked her dead in the eyes, and burst out in laughter.

"Let's go," I said to Ralph

Mom always told me to never let someone who is miserable steal your happy. Ignore them and move on.

I was having a great day that day, and she was not going to take my happy.

Today, I had no happy within me.

"I heard that you and Brian are no longer an item." She smirks. "I could never understand why he was so hung up on you."

"I never knew we were an item before," I reply. Staring in her eyes, I shake my head, then survey the hallway for an escape away from these fools.

"He came to his senses and made the better choice. Too bad you don't have a date to prom," she says sarcastically as she and her followers trot down the hallway giggling.

Rolling my eyes, I continue on to the parking lot thinking this day can't end fast enough.

The car ride home is quiet. By my demeanor, Tinea knows I'm not up for conversation. I thank her for the ride and run upstairs to my apartment. I drop my book bag by the door, kick off my shoes, and trudge into the kitchen. I open the freezer, digging through the packages of meats in search for a tub of pistachio ice cream. I throw my hands up, screaming to the heavens. There is no ice cream to be found. Feeling defeated, I fall to the ground and cry.

I empty my vessel of all the liquid I can through my tear ducts. I retract myself from the kitchen and walk to the bathroom, deciding that a shower will help me feel anything but dark and gray.

I turn the shower knob to the hottest temperature I

can get. I lazily remove my clothing. Looking up at mirror, I don't recognize the person looking back at me. My skin is pale, my eyes are red and puffy with black streaks of mascara running down my face.

You look like hell.

Turning away from the mirror, I enter the shower. The scalding hot water is a welcome reprieve.

With comfort in mind, I get dressed in my favorite white U2 shirt and gray sweatpants. Not wanting to catch a cold, I return to the bathroom, gather my hairbrush and blow dryer, partially drying my hair. I run my hands through my hair, ensuring I've removed all the knots with my brush. Once I'm satisfied, I reach for the black hair tie from the corner of the bathroom sink. I gather my hair and place it in messy bun.

The sudden rumbling in my stomach reminds me that I haven't eaten today.

On the way to the kitchen, I'm greeted by my book bag and Converse shoes that are thrown haphazardly throughout the living room.

If Mom walked in to this mess, let's just say that my day would get worse than it is now.

We don't have much. We live in an eight-hundred-square feet, two-bedroom, one bathroom apartment. The apartment is small but never cluttered and always clean. Everything has its place. She can't afford elegant vases, furniture, or knick-knacks. All we have is the brown love seat, a maple wood frame chair covered with a blue tattered cushion on top, and a worn-out wood coffee table which we have painted espresso twice.

The white walls are sparely decorated with photos of me. We have an eat-in kitchen, with a small two seat chipped bistro table. All furnishings were bought from the Goodwill in Lake Worth.

Our apartment has a balcony with a quaint red chair that overlooks the parking lot instead of the Atlantic Ocean.

Mom stresses that although it seems like we don't have a lot, we are blessed with plenty.

I get the items off the living room floor, retrieve my cellphone, and return to the kitchen for something to eat.

I remember the two-day-old meat lovers pizza in the refrigerator. Grabbing the last two slices, I pop them into the microwave.

I don't know how people eat cold pizza. I shake my head, that's just nasty.

I snag a can of Pepsi, plop down at the rectangular table in to kitchen, and begin devouring the pizza while scrolling through my phone for any missed texted messages.

Although pizza is always my first food of choice, today it tastes like cardboard.

As I place another slice of pizza to my mouth, my phone rings.

It's Ryan.

"Hi," I answer.

"Hey."

"Are you finished with practice already?" I can hear the melody of his Porsche through the phone.

"Yeah, we have a game tomorrow. Coach let us out early to rest up. We are playing Franklin Prep; that will be an easy win."

"Okay."

"Did you speak with that guy yet?"

I shake my head in response, but remember that he can't see me.

"Yeah," I sniffle.

"Are you crying?" he asks, a hint of worry in his voice.

"No," I reply too quickly.

"What's wrong then? You sound a bit off."

"Nothing," I lie. "Can I give you a call back later?"

"Why?"

"Just later, okay? Bye," I say as I hang up.

Appetite ruined, I get up and toss what's left of my pizza in the garbage bin.

Moving to the living room, I curl up on the brown couch with the remote in hand and turn on the TV.

Today is the perfect day to veg out and watch my favorite cartoon.

Lost in the world of Pinky and the Brain, I jump from the couch when I'm startled by the doorbell.

I'm not expecting a visitor, and no one normally comes to my house unannounced. I walk to the door and stand on the tips of my toes to see who it is through the peek hole.

I'm surprised to see Ryan standing on the other side.

I run my hand through my hair, removing the hair tie.

What's the point of trying to look presentable when I feel like shit anyway?

I open the front door. "What are you doing here?"

"Something is wrong with you."

I look to the floor as the tears begin to run down my cheeks again.

Ryan gently pulls me to him and encircles me in his arms. He rubs my back in a circular motion. My tears seem endless.

Stepping back, he holds my chin up as his mouth captures mine.

"Go get your shoes," he beckons.

I walk swiftly to my closet, grabbing my old faithful Converse and my keys.

He stands closely behind me as I lock the front door. Ryan holds my hand down the stairs to his Porsche parked in the guest spot. He holds the passenger door open and waits until I'm seated before jogging around to the driver's side.

He drives to the Valley Memorial Park two miles away from my home.

Valley Memorial Park has a magnificent two-foot-wide man-made waterfall surrounded by sweet, colorful smelling plants. The water pounds the rocks, spurting over into the clear water below.

"It's so beautiful," I say as we sit on the bench gazing at the waterfall.

"It sure is."

He gently turns my head away from the waterfall, staring in my eyes.

I know the question is coming before he can even utter a word.

"I want to know why you were crying earlier."

"It was a horrible day."

Looking down, I fold my hands in my lap. "I hurt Brian today, and I feel horrible," I whisper.

"It will be okay, Sim. You have a good soul, and that's why you feel the way you do now. People have a right to change their mind at any time." Looking down at me, he asks, "Do you regret changing your mind?"

I hesitate as I contemplate my reply. Do I regret it?

His face becomes tense, brows knitted.

"No, I don't regret it."

I don't regret it, I regret the delivery and timing but not the chance to be with Ryan.

"Good," he states, grinning. His emerald greens eyes sparkle with delight.

We spend the rest of the time making plans for prom.

Chapter Ten

It's chaotic this morning in the Lopez/Goodman household. So many appointments, so little time. Manicure, pedicure, and eyebrows at 9:30 a.m., hair washed, blown, and styled at 12:30 p.m. and professional makeup at 5:30 p.m.

Mom stands over the stove with a spatula in one hand, waiting to flip the pancake in the frying pan. The sizzling bacon arouses the hunger in my stomach.

Walking over to Mom, I place a kiss to her cheek. "Morning."

"Hi, sweetheart, big day today."

The feeling of delirious happiness and anxiety zips through my body all at once.

It's the day of the prom.

Mom still believes that Brian will be escorting me.

Who would think I wouldn't be able to share this process in my life with her? Subconsciously, I'd rather Mom not knowing about Ryan and I.

How would she see our relationship? Would she think it's inappropriate?

I am dating the son of her employer.

This secret, for now, is probably for the best.

With plate in hand, I grab a pancake, a strip of bacon, and a glass of orange juice from the counter.

With only fifteen minutes to spare, I gobble my breakfast, then retrieve my mom's car keys from the key holder by the front door.

I return home at 3:30 p.m.

I take my black duffle bag from the closet, placing it on my bed. Turning to the espresso dresser, I open the drawer, removing a powder blue bra with a frilly panty set, black jeans, and a pink tank top. I take off my Converse and place them with the items I gathered in to the bag.

Tapping my index finger against my cheek, I ponder, "What else?" I snap my fingers. I forgot to pack my toiletries.

I glance through my overnight bag a third time, ensuring that I have all I needed for my adventure later tonight. Once satisfied, I zip my duffle bag closed.

I place a shower cap meticulously over my hair before hopping into the shower. I'd be livid if I messed up my hair that took hours to accomplish.

After the shower, I lotion and spray my body twice with vanilla scented body spray from head to toe. Wrapping myself back in my bathrobe, I sit on my bed, waiting for the makeup artist to arrive.

Two hour and ten minutes later, makeup completed and dressed. I stand in front of the floor-to-wall mirror in awe of the strange girl reflecting back at me. Tears well in my eyes. I fan my face to the stop the tears from falling.

Walking down the narrow hallway to the living room, I'm stopped by Mom's excitement.

"Oh My Gosh, Simone," Mom screams at the top of her lungs, tears flowing down her face.

"Gorgeous," Uncle Sam states, standing from the couch.

I twirl around, showing off all angles of my outfit.

From the makeup on my face, to the dress and the shoes. I know it's corny to say, but I feel like a princess.

55

My makeup is light and dewy. The kohl wing tipped eyeliner, layered mascara, and shimmering golden and black smokey halo on my almond eyes is done perfectly. The apples of my cheeks accentuated the shade of apricot. It's topped off with lips of sin.

Tinea arrives at my home at 7:00 p.m. Mom takes a couple pictures of us, then we take the twenty-minute journey to downtown West Palm Beach.

The prom is being held at the Smithson Convention Center. The prom's theme, "fairytale" is such a metaphor for my life at the moment.

The closer we get to downtown, the more nauseous I become. Clenching my lips together, I hold my breath, counting to ten.

That doesn't help to settle my nerves.

Closing my eyes, I breathe in my nose and exhale out my mouth a few times.

That's no use.

I twiddle my thumbs.

"Will you calm down? You look gorgeous. He is going to want to hold on to you all night," Tinea encourages.

Comforting words from a friend; that doesn't work. My insides are still in knots.

I'm not only worried about what Ryan will think of my appearance. I am worried that he may not show up. We haven't spoke at all, today.

I would be mortified.

Karma wouldn't be that cruel, right?

There are droves of cars at the convention center. As we drive around searching for a parking space, I spot Ryan leaning on the hood of his Porsche.

Upon seeing him, the nausea becomes a fleeting rain.

"Did you see that guy standing next the Porsche?" Tinea questions as drool runs out the side of her mouth.

"Yeah, what about him?" Back the hell off, heffa.

"I don't think he goes to our school, have you seen him before?"

"No, I haven't seen him around school." Why is she trembling? "There's a spot."

Please don't tell me she has a crush on him.

"He's hot. I need a closer look," she says as we exit the car.

A beautiful symphony begins playing in my stomach the closer I get to Ryan.

He leans against the car, ankles crossed, with his hands in his black suit pants. He has on a crisp, white shirt and skinny, mustard tie to match my dress.

He turns his head, and as our eyes meet, fireworks explode.

He smiles from ear-to-ear. The emotion is reciprocated.

"Love the hair. Nice, kissable lips," she whispers.

Slowly, he begins walking toward me as I continue my walk toward him.

"You know him?" Tinea asks, biting her lip.

"Baby, you're looking so gorgeous. WOW!" he states as he stands, looking down at me.

He lowers his head so our faces are level and pulls me in to a fervent kiss.

As we pull away slowly, air escapes between my swollen lips. I wave my hands at my face to cool down the heat that's leaving my body.

I forgot about my best friend. Turning to Tinea, her mouth is dropped open as she stares back and forth at us.

"Ryan, this is my best friend, Tinea. Tinea this is my Ryan."

"Wow," she replies.

Laughing, I nudge her with my shoulder.

"Nice to meet you," she says to Ryan as she stretches forth her hand.

"You too," he replies, shaking her hand firmly.

His brows rise. "My Ryan? I love the sound of that." He places a kiss on my forehead.

Rubbing his hands with a smirk on his face, he turns to us. "Ladies, I think it's time to get this party started."

Chapter Eleven

Our hands are intertwined as we enter the building. Tinea's date, Tony Parizza, is waiting in the lobby, wearing a white suit with a sky-blue vest.

Tinea introduces Tony to Ryan, and they seem to hit it off. I was skeptical that Tony would be rude to Ryan since Brian and Tony are teammates.

The facility is huge, divided into several conference rooms. As we proceed down the hall, we come upon a sign adjacent to the third door on the left that reads "A STARRY NIGHT. WELCOME TO ROYAL PALM HIGH, JUNIOR PROM."

A thrill sweeps through my body. I can't wait to see the decorations, dance, and have fun with this guy next to me.

"WOW!" I whisper, blown away by the decorations in the room. The prom committee did a spectacular job.

We follow Tinea and Tony over to a group of friends that are lounging at one of the many tables. I make formal introductions of Ryan to everyone. The boys start discussing some sports, and the girls talk about the journey it took for us to get here tonight.

I snap my fingers and shimmy my shoulders as Usher's "My Way" blasts through the speakers.

"You want to dance?" Ryan whispers in my ear.

I nod in reply.

"We will be back," he announces to the table, taking

my hands in his.

The glow exuding from me is blinding.

Finding our spot on the dance floor, I wrap my hands around his neck, and he places his hands around my waist as we danced to the music. We get lost in the music, song after song, intertwined together. Our gazes remain locked. His emerald eyes enthrall me. I suck air through my lips. My breathing becomes labored. He slides his hands down and rests them on my butt. Our swaying intensifies into a slow grind.

"All right, Royal Palm High," a voice echoes from the mic, breaking our trance.

Applause rings out.

Standing on the dance floor listening to Chris on the mic, I get the sense that I'm being watched. I glance around the room, meeting eyes with surprise, curiosity, and envy staring at us.

"Let's go back to the table," I say.

He gives an approving nod.

I slant my chair behind Ryan, shielding myself from all the inquisitive looks.

Did they believe I couldn't get a date?

Are they staring at Ryan?

Peeking around Ryan's back, I searched for Suzen; Ms. Head Cheerleader is looking at Ryan in awe and shock.

Yeah, bitch, only thing you can do is look.

"Hey what are you doing back there?"

I jump

"Nothing."

"You want to go back out?"

Clearing my throat, I respond. "Not yet. I am a bit thirsty though."

"I will be right back."

I smile, wiggling my fingers.

Suzen chooses this moment to invade our group with Brian's arm slung around her shoulder.

"Hi, guys." She waves.

A few from the table reply.

Turning to me, she snarls. "Wow, you look different."

I don't know if that was an actual compliment. If it was, it would be a first. She can't fool me. I know her better than that.

I grin and cock my head to the side. "In what way do I look different?"

"You actually look like a girl," she laughs.

Why is this witch trying to ruin the night for me? I see myself stepping out of my leopard heels and jabbing her.

At least I am not dressed for an audition at the Spearmint Club.

"A gorgeous girl," Ryan says, handing me a drink. His emeralds are frosty as he looks up at Suzen. Jaw tense, he continues to stare at her. "Ugly doesn't look good on you."

Brian walks off, and Suzen remains rooted with her mouth open, ready to receive flies.

The table erupts in laughter. Ryan grabs my hands and guides me back onto the dance floor.

We dance, and dance, and dance, wrapped up in each other's arms. Tinea and I scream and dance when our favorite song is played. They guys shake their heads like we're crazy.

To no surprise, Brian and Suzen are named prom king and queen. They deserve each other; actually, Brian deserves better.

I just cannot bring myself to like her.

After accepting her crown, she turns to me and jeers.

You got a crown, and I got the hottest guy in the building.

I clap and cheer the loudest.

Tinea looks at me, puzzled. Shaking her head, she asks, "What the hell!?"

I see that Suzen is threatened by me. I just don't understand why. She is considered to be the most beautiful girl in the school. She is captain of the cheerleading squad, and head of the student counsel. She dresses in the latest designer labels, drives a Lexus, and her makeup, nails, and hair are always perfect.

While I wear t-shirts, jeans, and Converse. My hair is always in a pony tail, and I wear no makeup except for mascara and lip gloss.

I go to school to simply learn and get the grades to get into Baker University.

It's a conundrum.

After two and a half of hours of utter enjoyment, minus the minor infraction, we exit the Smithson Convention Center.

I walk with Tinea and Tony to grab my overnight bag from her car while Ryan gets his car.

"Where are you guys going?"

I can see the wheels turning in her head. I never spoke to her about the conversation Ryan and I had a few days ago.

"Why are you acting so weird?" Ryan questioned.

I huffed. "I'm not acting weird."

"Answer the question: Have you ever had sex?"

"No! Have you?"

"Once, or a couple of times. Does it matter?"

A sudden black cloud covered me.

Did it matter knowing that he had been with different girls?

"I guess it does ..." Why wouldn't it? I have been pondering having him be my first. That's special, my virginity has value.

Biting my index finger, I wondered how he would feel if the roles were reversed.

"Does it matter if I had sex before?"

"Hmmm ... I don't think so, probably, probably not," he mumbled. "I am very excited that I will be your first and only."

"Soooo ... How many girls have you been with?" I slapped my hand to my forehead. I didn't mean to ask that question out loud. I have no sense of self preservation. "Don't answer that," I yelled. I didn't want to be tormented by that information.

The sound of relief echoed through the phone.

"I want to spend prom night with you. What do you think about that?" he asked in a husky tone.

I have never spent the night with a guy. My entire body quivered, the thought of it was exhilarating.

"I would like that."

Shrugging my shoulders, I stare Tinea in the eyes. "I have no clue."

Ryan drives up alongside Tinea's car with a smile that makes me laugh. He jogs around the car, taking my bag and placing it in the trunk.

"Nice car," Tony states with envy.

"Ah, it's alright." Ryan shrugs.

We say our goodbyes. I strap myself in the passenger seat of the car as he speeds away.

Chapter Twelve

The car cruises west on Okeechobee Blvd then merges onto I-95 Miami ramp.

Where in the world are we going?

I have been trying to get it out of him to no avail.

Ryan slyly places his hand on my exposed thigh, causing a tingle through my body.

His touch abates my curiosity of where we were heading.

At eighty miles per hour, the silver Porsche sails past Boynton Beach, Delray Beach, Boca Raton, Fort Lauderdale, North Miami, and proceeds down the highway.

Where in the hell are we heading?

I knit my brows, peaking at him from the corner of my eye. He rubs his index finger in the middle of my brows. His deep laughter fills the car.

"It's driving you crazy, isn't it?"

"What's driving me crazy?"

"Not knowing where we are going."

I shake my head, laughing. "It's not driving me crazy!"

"You're not a good liar, Simone."

"I'm not lying. I am passed being crazy. I am going insane trying to figure it out. Each time I think I have resolved your little mystery, we pass the exit."

Taking my hand in his, he kisses the middle of my palm. "We are almost there."

Ten minutes later, we exit at E/Miami Beach. The car continues east, nothing but water in sight.

My cheeks swell at the surprise. We are parked right outside the Lewis Miami Beach Hotel.

"South Beach." It took one and half hours, but it was worth it.

"South Beach." He winks.

Ryan goes to check us in while I admire the lobby.

I ponder why Ryan choose a place all the way in South Beach. Don't get me wrong, I am elated. I mean it's South Beach. We passed two counties to get here, and it's only for one night.

Is he worried about people finding out? I know we discussed his mom not knowing.

Save the inner monologue for another day, Simone. Just enjoy the night.

I shake myself and stare at the man walking toward me.

He grabs our overnight bags that are next to my feet. "Let's go." He inclines his head toward the elevators.

Ryan walks into the suite, through the living room into what I assume to be the bedroom with our bags.

"What do you think?" he asks, leaning against the bedroom doorframe.

I open my mouth, but the words escape me. How do I describe this opulent suite?

Ryan walks up to me, taking my hands in his, and leads me through the bedroom to the balcony.

"If inside leaves you speechless, wait until you see this."

My eyes round at the picturesque view before me. White, twinkling light dust across the black canvas. The silver glow of the moonlight illuminates the ripples and crashes of the endless miles of dark water.

The electricity in the air intensifies.

Ryan wraps his hands around my waist from behind. I leaned into the comfort of his body, getting lost in the moment. He dips his head down, resting his chin on my shoulder as he tightens his hold.

I tilt my head as he rains kisses along my neck. A long breath escapes me. He gently turns my head and captures my mouth in his.

Liquid pours from my core, soaking my panties.

His left-hand travels from my waist to the apex of my thighs. I widen my legs, grinding into him. I gasp at the size of him.

In a split second, his thumb circles my bean.

I moan into his mouth, exhaling a desperation I have never felt before. Something starts building inside of me.

I can't believe I am on the verge of my first orgasm.

Abruptly, he lifts his mouth from mine. I open my eyes, looking into his darkened orbs.

His finger slips inside my panties. He continues his administration, eliciting whimpers.

"Has anyone every touched you here?" he growls in my ear.

"No," I breathlessly reply.

He pulls out. My body cries out at the loss of his touch.

He slowly pulls the zipper of my aurora borealis rhinestone, yellow, one shoulder, chiffon gown down my back, as he traces kisses along my spine.

I tremble with need.

He taps my leg. "Step out of the dress."

I am left standing on the balcony in nothing but my skimpy panties.

He throws me over his shoulder, carries me to bed, and lays me down. He steps back, my legs spread apart. His eyes smolder as he lazily appraises me.

He removes his shirt, revealing that washboard stomach I constantly dream of caressing. Slowly, he removes his belt, unbuttons his pants and stands in nothing but Calvin Klein. The moonlight spills onto his naked chest and shoulders. It disarms me, seeing him like this.

The soothing crashes of the waves contradict with the djembe drums beating in me.

He prowls toward the bed. Climbing on top of me, his lips find mine. This kiss is like no other we've had before. It holds a hunger, causing the djembe to beat louder.

He nips at my tongue and my lips with his teeth. Growling as he kisses down my neck. He wraps his mouth around my breast, alternating between sucking, biting, and stroking them. My pebbles hardened more.

I wriggle on the bed from the constant pleasurable torture.

He growls, "Stop moving."

I clench the sheet with both hands to secure me.

He continues kissing down my stomach, moving lower, and lower. I gasp as he kisses between my thighs.

I slither on the bed, unable to control the sensations jolting through my body. He's doing things with his tongue I have only read about.

I grip his dark mane with both hands. My head falls back. I'm panting loudly. My leg trembles. A flame is building inside me.

An unexpected cry escapes me as tremors wrack my body.

I lay still, eyes closed, drained, and gasping for breath.

"You okay?"

I open my eyes. "Yep."

A satisfied smile is on his face. He picks up a condom and rips it open with his teeth. I watch with deep concern as he pulls it down his penis.

He bends over me, kissing me. Gazing into each other's eyes, he says, "It will always be me."

Chapter Thirteen

The following month goes by in a daze. I spend most weekends with Ryan. We never stay locally, always worried that we will get caught. There's a thrill that goes through me each weekend.

The freedom is intoxicating. I am always seen as the good girl. I always do what I'm told, follow the straight and narrow line set before me. I don't go to parties or drink like my peers. I get good grades. I was a virgin. I am boring.

Now, each weekend I have something exciting to look forward to. I never know where we will end up. We travel to Orlando, Tampa, Key West. All places I have never been, and the accommodations are stunning.

My mom still has no clue that I'm spending my weekends naked with Ryan between my legs. Thinking instead that I'm with Tinea. Thank God she isn't friendly with Tinea's parents. They met once—let's just say they didn't blend.

I feel guilty lying to my mom, but deep down I know that she won't approve of my relationship with Ryan.

After all, he is the boss's son. I am the forbidden fruit.

April 20th, we find ourselves on Sanibel Island. Ryan's eighteenth birthday weekend.

We spend the Saturday lounging on the beach and

collecting seashells.

While Ryan is in the shower, I finish getting ready for dinner. I slip into a short, black, slip dress courtesy of Tinea. I bend over, putting on the red, Prada,strappy heals-another item from Tinea.

"Don't fucking move."

His hand wraps around my waist, picking me up over his shoulder. My nipples go erect at the sound of his gruff voice.

I land on the bed, bouncing at the force in which he threw me. I giggle as he lays above me, roaring. Ryan buries his hand in my hair as he pushes his tongue into my mouth.

I pull the towel away from his waist, revealing a body that an eighteen-year-old shouldn't have. A chest with a six-pack that narrows down to a slender waist. My panties are soaked. I need him. NOW.

His right hand slides under my barely there dress. He taps my thigh. "Lift."

I raise my hips off the bed as he slowly drags my wet panties down my leg.

"This is going to be quick and hard, baby."

I cry out as he roughly enters me. He grumbles in pleasure.

Not to be outdone, I meet him thrust for thrust. He sucks hard on my bottom lip.

I hiss.

The pleasure is too much to bear. I relax and let go.

I lay across his chest, eyes closed, wrapped in the afterglow of our love making. Ryan lazily runs his hand through my hair.

"Hungry?"

"Starved."

There's a bite in the night air. I shiver, climbing the

stairs to Blue's, the famous seafood restaurant.

Ryan groans. "Fuck."

"What is it?"

"We've got to go." He turns, dragging me back the way we came.

"What's wrong?"

"I spotted the Mikolic's. They're friends with Mom."

"That was close." I sigh. "Burger King instead of crab legs?"

"Not just any burger, babe. A Whopper with bacon and cheese." He grins.

I sit on my couch, finishing my English paper that's due on Friday. Unable to concentrate, I drift off, thinking of the weekend on Sanibel Islands. I get so wrapped up in the moments that we are together, my body willows when we are apart, counting the minutes to another weekend.

I shake my head. *You need to get it together, Simone. It's only been two days.*

A chime echoes in the living room. I reach for my phone sitting on the coffee table. The notification show's a text from Ryan.

Ri: Where are you?

Sim: Home, trying to finish this English paper that's due Friday.

Ri: Practice got out early. I'm coming to get you. We are going to my house.

Sim: Is that the best idea?

Ri: Yeah, I need to get out of this uniform, and you can help me study for this math test tomorrow. Better part: I don't have to wait until the weekend to see you.

Sim: Okay.

Ri: I'll let you know when I'm there.

I shove my book and laptop in my bag. I trip over the coffee table as I get off the couch. I laugh out loud.

That's what you get for getting too excited.

I take off my gray shorts and pull on my blue jean skirt. I take my hair out of it's pony tail, run my hand through it a couple times, and apply two coats of my BonBon pink lip gloss.

I walk down the hallway, then make a u-turn back into my room, digging through the closet trying to find my black cardigan.

Mom would lose her marbles if she saw me in this tank top with nothing covering it.

Cardigan in hand, my phone chimes. Taking the phone out of my back pocket, I see the message.

Ri: I'm here.

I place a quick kiss on his lips as I slip inside his new, midnight blue Range Rover. A birthday gift from his parents. He jokes that he's just getting a jump start on his car collection.

I pull my hands from his as we approach the black, wrought iron gate.

Ryan runs upstairs to change out of his clothing and grab his math supplies.

I put my hands through the sleeve of the cardigan as I make my way to the kitchen in search of my mom. I search the laundry room, movie room, and Mr. Mulligan's office.

I narrow my eyes.

Where could she be? I'm not going upstairs.

Returning to the kitchen, I decide to wait there for Ryan.

I jump, startled by the slap on my left butt cheek. Ryan kisses me on the forehead, quiet laughter in his eyes.

"Do you want a slice of key lime pie?"

I nod and rub my hands together. Key lime pie is my third love. First is mom's apple pie, then sweet potato pie, followed by key lime pie.

Ryan opens the left kitchen cabinet, taking a dessert plate and glass. He pours a glass of lemonade and starts to slice a piece of pie.

"This big enough?"

I shake my head no.

He widens the knife. Raises his eyebrows.

I nod.

I trail him to the library. I lick my lips in admiration of how low his sweatpants ride his waist. That tight ass. I just want to grab it.

Yum. A cheesy smile lights on my face.

Throwing caution to the wind, I straddle Ryan as he sits on the love seat.

His eyes widen.

We feed each other pie, lemonade, and pecks on the lips until all traces of the pie are gone.

He glares at me with a silent challenge.

I cock my eyebrow.

I slip my hands around his neck and grind against him.

He groans and captures my mouth in his.

I gasp as his hand trailed up my stomach, under my bra to pluck to my nipple.

The need to have him inside me flames. I have

become a sex monster. I grind down harder against his erection.

"What the hell is going on in here?" a voice screeches.

I jolt from Ryan's lap at the sound of Mrs. Mulligan's voice.

"Oh my God!" I whisper, hands shaking. I hang my head down, looking at the maple wood floor.

I am so stupid. Why did you sit in his lap? Why did you feel so brazen?

I push away Ryan's hand as he tries to clasp mine. I slid further away from him.

"Simone, stop!" he whisper-yells.

I slowly lift my head and am met with the death glare from Mrs. Mulligan's infuriated face.

I glance at Ryan. He steps next to me, firmly clasping my hands in his.

"Don't pull away," he growls, staring coldly at his mom.

I release a harsh breath. *This is not going to end well.* Dread builds in the pit of stomach.

"Mom."

"Don't mom me," she yells. "What the hell is going on here?" She points between us.

"I was just making out with my girlfriend."

"You're what?" she screams.

If only I could just disappear. Poof.

Mom halts as she crashes the door of the library open. "What in the world is all this yelling about?"

Mom's face hardens at the picture we painted before her.

"What's going on here, you two?" she asks, with her hands on her waist.

"That's exactly what I am trying to find out. I found

74

them in here, humping each other." Distain is written on her face.

I am not good enough for her son. I am not wanted.

I try to pull my hands away. Ryan tightens his hold.

I turn to him, pleading with my eyes to let me go.

He looks at me and shakes his head.

Walking towards us, wagging her fingers, Mrs. Mulligan says, "Ryan, let her go this instant. This is not happening."

"What!?"

"Over my dead body."

He drops my hands as he storms up to his mom, yelling.

I squeeze my eyes shut, hoping to stop the tears.

I hurry passed my mom, out the library, and run out the front door.

Chapter Fourteen

I walk around in circles outside in the driveway. Mom doesn't get off work for couple of hours. I dial Tinea's number again, still no answer.

How am I going to get out of here?

The front door opens. I look away from my phone into the eyes of anger and utter disappointment.

I look away, not able to handle the emotions.

"Let's go," Mom says, moving toward her old, white, Toyota Corolla.

I walked to the car with trepidation in my heart. As much fun as I've been having with Ryan, it isn't worth the pain I hear in my mom's voice.

Oh my gosh! I hope I didn't get her fired.

I open the passenger door and sit in the car. My hand stills on the door handle as Ryan dashes through the front door.

"Wait, Rose, I can take Simone home," he says out loud, walking toward me.

Mom holds her hand out as she exits the car. "Ryan, not right now. I need to have a talk with my daughter. Thanks for the offer, but …" She shakes her head, and enters the car.

"I do care for Simone, Rose. This is not a game for me."

Mom puts the car in reverse, backing the car out of the Mulligans' gate.

I swallow. Tears shower down my cheeks. Ryan

watches us leaving. I study his face. He's pissed.

The thick silence in the car chills me; a looming fear that comes with the murky afternoon. Stony, gray clouds opens up, weeping with me.

The thrill of the unknown is now replaced with fear. The high I have been in dissolves. I shiver, hoping and praying that I can find a way to fix this.

I don't know what to say to my mom. I can beg for forgiveness. I knew, yeah, I knew that his mom wouldn't approve of us. Subconsciously that's why I agreed with Ryan to hide our relationship. I knew she would see me as lesser.

I run through the rain, up the stairs. My clothes are soaked from the downpour. The closer I get to the front door, the harder I cry. I dig into my bag and take out the keys. They clatter to the ground as I fumble to insert them into the door.

I huff. I bend, picking the keys off the floor.

"Move, Simone, I will open the door," my mom says, closing her umbrella.

I back away from the door and stand with my arms hugging me.

"Get in," Mom yells.

I jump.

The door slams behind us.

With my head down, I walk toward my room.

"Where are you going?"

I sniff and whisper, "To my room."

"No, you need to explain what the hell has been going on with you and Ryan."

I look at her, dumbfounded. *How am I going to explain this?*

"Hmm…"

"When did this all start?" she asks as she takes her shoes off.

77

"A couple weeks after I began tutoring him."

"Why didn't you tell me? This is my job. He's my employer's son. What were you thinking!?" I know she's agitated. I can see her hands moving around from the corner of my eye.

Staring at the beaten, brown carpet is better than seeing the disappointment etched on her face.

I shrug. "Mom, we love each other," I whisper.

"Love!" she scoffs. "You two know nothing about love. Lust, yes. Love, no."

"How can you say that!?" I yell.

"'Cause you don't know what love is, Simone." She shakes her head and points her finger at me. "You are too young. You think what you feel is love. It's not! It's infatuation. It's the excitement of being with the person you never thought would want you."

She doesn't understand. I shake my head.

"It's more than that." I raise my hand, wiping snot into the elbow of my cardigan.

"No, Mija, it's not."

I pace around in the confined hallway. My breathing shallows.

"I know because I felt exactly the same way about your dad." Her words still my movement. Placing her finger under my chin, she lifts my head and places her hands on my cheeks.

"Look at me."

I see the depth of pain that sits deep behind her orbs.

"Your dad was it for me. He was my everything. I couldn't believe that he would want me. The girl who didn't have the right last name. Who wasn't from a prominent family. His family tried to dissuade him from choosing me. I thought he loved me for me. I had a thick veil covering my eyes when it came to him. I never saw the signs that everyone warned me of. In the end, he chose his family over me. He left."

My eyes well. "Mom, don't you think I realize that? He didn't just leave you. He left me too. He started a new family. He abandoned me. I am nothing to him. My own dad couldn't love me. How must another man love me?"

"Oh my God! Baby, no."

She wraps her arms around me. I lay my head on her chest and sob.

"It's what it is, Mom," I mumble.

I pull away, emotionally drained from the left turn the afternoon took. I take a quick shower, grab a pair of blue, tattered pajama shorts and a matching top, and crawl into bed.

I'm seething at the thought that my mom might be right about me and Ryan. Maybe, just maybe, I was living in wunderland. I was only seventeen. *What do you really know about love?* A sharp pain hits me. I rub my hand over the upper left side of my chest, trying to alleviate it.

Never give a man your all. *Never give a man the power to hurt you.*

A short beep shatters my inner monologue. I turn on my side, facing the window, ignoring the continuous beeps coming from my phone.

Wet tears appear on the pink bed sheet as I silently weep, unsure of what will be.

Chapter Fifteen

It's been nine days.

Each morning, a ray of sunshine trails me until it wanes into my monochrome, damp, frigid existence. It takes nine days to sew up the small gashes in my soul. Nine days to rid me of the longing and the pain that's too much to deal with. At night, it feels too hard to cope; the darkness my blanket of protection.

Thoughts of missed Christmases, birthdays, Father's days, and daddy daughter dances. I try hard to escape it. For nine days, the nothingness resides in me, munching until it gets it fill.

Nine days ignoring Ryan's calls and texts. Nine days to fortify my heart.

Day ten, I wake fully armored.

Mom stands by the kitchen counter eating a toasted bagel with cream cheese.

"Morning."

She laughs. "She speaks."

"How has work been?" I ask, not so much for her but wanting to get information on Ryan. I slice a cinnamon bagel, placing it into the toaster. I lean back against the counter nonchalantly.

She squints her eyes. "The boy has lost his mind. He is driving me nuts. Walking around the place brooding. He hasn't spoken to his mother in nine days."

She washes off her plate, placing it in the

dishwasher. She grabs her purse off the counter and heads to the door. With her hand on the doorknob, she turns to me with a solemn look.

She sighs. "Call the boy." Then she leaves.

The bagel pops up; I slather it with cream cheese. My phone beeps a message from Tinea that she's downstairs.

The nine days didn't only affect me, but everyone surrounding me. I hardly spoke or answered with only one word. At lunch, I stared off into the depth of my subconscious. At home, my room was my refuge.

I told Tinea about my non-existing relationship with my dad. She was aware of my battles.

Ha … let's call it what it is: depression. During my bouts, she stays far but close enough for me to lean.

"Hey." I smile as I entered her car.

"She smiles." She waves her hands in the air. "My girl is back."

I giggle.

"Have you spoken to Ryan yet?"

I shake my head no.

"What are you waiting for? I have seen the missed calls on your phone."

I glance at her. "Nosy bitch. What were you doing with my phone?"

"It kept going off. It was annoying the hell out of me."

"Ha."

I open my phone and begin reading my text messages.

RI: Babe, answer the phone.

Ri: Sim, please answer the phone.

Ri: I spoke with my parents about us. Mom has her own agenda. I don't care what she thinks or

has to say. Dad he gets it though. He knows I am serious about us.

Ri: I miss you.

Ri: Please call me back or answer the phone.

Ri: I miss you.

Ri: I spoke to your mom today.

Ri: Morning, I love you. I miss you. I miss seeing you. I miss touching you.

I itched to answer my phone each time it chimed or a notification showed a missed text with his name. Each time, I bite my lip until the taste of sweet crimson sits on my tongue.

Sim: I miss you too. Morning. My index finger hovers over the send button.

Send it, Simone, just be careful. Don't give your all.

I press send.

Ryan comes to my house after school that afternoon. I open the front door and pause, staring into the emeralds I haven't seen in ten days.

I step aside to let him in, then close the door. I turn around and run into his solid chest.

"I've missed you," he says. He wraps his arms around me.

My heart swells. "I've missed you too."

He steps back and takes a seat on the couch.

I walk over to the blue chair, sitting cross-legged.

Looking me in the eye, Ryan smiles. "I have missed those lips."

"Really." I laugh. I'm anxious.

"Yeah, really. Before I kiss them, we need to talk about what was going on these past ten days. Why were you mad with me? Do you not want us anymore?"

I have never had the conversation with Ryan about my dad. He knew that my dad wasn't in my life, but I have never gone into detail about the effects it has on me emotionally and mentally.

We talk through the sunset. I cry. He looks at me with pity. I yell. We laugh and decide to take a day at a time. We decide to mingle our worlds, no more hiding. Saturday, we would meet each other's crews.

I'm giddy with excitement. My smile grows as time draws closer for us to meet with Ryan and his friends.

I made plans to get dressed with Tinea and meet Ryan with his friends at City Place Cheesecake Factory for dinner. Based on how the dinner goes, we may see a movie afterward. We planned on there being ten people total.

My crew consists of two people: Tinea and Tony.

I didn't need to lie to Mom this time. The only drawback is the eleven o'clock curfew.

I walk out of Tinea's ensuite bathroom, towel wrapped on my head and around my body.

I sit on her purple, king size bed with the Jergens body lotion.

"What are you wearing tonight, girly?" Tinea asks walking out of her walk-in closet with a raspberry, red, skater dress.

It's hot. The dress has a deep v in the front, lace bodice, sheer skirting, with a crisscross opening in the back.

Where the hell did she think she was going? It's too much.

"I'm just going to pull on a pair of tight, black

83

jeans." I grab the other items from my bag. "With this black, faux leather corset. What do you think?" I bite my lip, waiting for her reply.

"Giiirrrlll … You are going to look like sex on wheels. I have the perfect red heels and gold accessories to go with that." She snaps her finger. "I am doing your hair and makeup. I'm thinking beach waves and edgier makeup."

"Okay. Something different. Let's do it." I burst with anticipation.

"What do you think of my dress?"

"Honestly, I love the dress. The dress is great." I place my fingers together. "It's a smidge too much."

"Well, I got to show out. Can't let these prep school snobs out dress me."

I laugh. "You are one of those rich kids, you just don't go to a prep school."

She pouts. "Yeah, but I ain't bougie."

She walks into her closet and returns dressed in sand washed jeans, a black tank, and a green army jacket.

"What now, bitch!"

"Perfect." I wink.

"Let's go. It's going to take me awhile to put you together."

"You wish."

We park the car at Macy's and begin our five-minute trot to the restaurant.

Ri: Where are you?
Sim: Walking to you now.

Turning the corner, I spot Ryan talking to a tall, blond guy. Adrenaline courses through my veins. I tingle all over.

I stop in my tracks at the cross walk. The blond guy

has his arm thrown around a girl's shoulder.

"OH MY GOSH!"

"What!?" Tinea asks, looking around.

"It's Madeline."

Chapter Sixteen

I watch as she throws her head back, erupting in laughter at whatever Ryan said. Although she's on the arm of another, she looks at Ryan with longing.

He turns, and our eyes meet. I smile and wave, even as my excitement starts to diminish at the sight of her. We stand waiting for the crosswalk signal to change.

Snap out of the funk. You got this.

The cross signal changes. I look fixedly at Ryan with lust filled eyes, swaying my hips, strutting across the crosswalk to him.

Hoping I don't look ridiculous.

He is rooted to the spot as he watches me. Ryan swallows, then licks his lips, fire smolders in his eyes.

That look only means one thing—he's hungry and it's not for cheesecake.

I mentally high five myself.

"Damn, baby," he says. I occupy his personal space.

"Hey." My lips lift upwards. The diminished excitement is reignited.

"You look sexy as fuck. Shit."

"You like?" I twirl around.

"I like and I hate it," he says, looking around. "All these dudes out here are looking at my stuff." He grabs my hips, bringing me to his side.

"Your stuff."

"Yeah." His mouth meets mine.

"Hey, dude, you coming up for air?" asks the blond guy.

We pull apart, smirking. I turn to Tinea, my cheeks the color of a red rose. I turn back to Ryan as he extends his middle finger to his friends.

I glance at Madeline. Her nostrils flare. I recognize pain in her eyes.

Ryan's crew consists of Bradley, the blond and best friend, Anthony, Carlos, and Mark. Anthony brought his girlfriend, Camille, and Bradley brought Madeline.

I will have to see what's up with Bradley and Madeline.

A hostess leads us to a rectangular table on the patio. Outside is cozy and warm, with an occasional mild wind.

Tony walks around the corner as we are being seated. Ryan and I sit in the middle, Tinea to my right, and Madeline across from me.

Lucky me.

I stare at Madeline, determined not to look away. I smile at her awkwardly. She smiles back insincerely. My smile falls as Madeline turned to Bradley.

Ryan sits, placing his arm behind my chair. His hand massages the back of my head.

I sag.

"What the hell is that witch's problem?" Tinea whispers in my ear. She points her chin toward Madeline.

I shrug. "I wish I knew."

She wants what she can't have.

"I am going to ask her if she looks at you like that again." Tinea stares at Madeline with a stink eye.

I smile and shake my head.

I'm surprised we're getting along as well as we are. Even with Madeline's snide remarks, I'm having fun.

We decide to have a couple slices of cheesecake before leaving.

"We are not going to make it to the movies," Ryan whispers and licks my ears.

"Really, why not?" I whisper.

A sly grin spreads across his face. He removes his hand from behind me, resting it on my thigh.

"You don't know how hard it has been sitting here through dinner. All I have been thinking about is the fastest way to get you out of that corset." He squeezes my thigh.

"Ohhh …" The tingly feeling starts again throughout my body.

"I can't believe summer break is within two weeks!" Madeline chimes in. "What do you guys have planned for the summer? Anything exciting, Simone?"

Ryan's circular motion on my thigh stills. The laughter evaporates from his eyes.

"No. What are your plans?" I ask, resting my elbows on the table.

"I am so excited!" She tosses her hair behind her. "I will be traveling Europe for the entire summer with my family and the Mulligans."

"Really? That should be something. Europe. Hopefully one day I will be able to go." I smile, hiding the hurt I feel.

I sit back and push Ryan's hand away from my thigh.

"Sim," he gently says.

"So, Bradley, what do you have planned? Anything as exciting as these two?" I point between Madeline and Ryan.

I drown out his reply. I can't put on my finger on what I am truly feeling. I don't know if I'm angry, disappointed, or jealous. His reaction means he already knew about this. When was he going to tell me?

I want to shout. I take a deep breath.

"Baby."

"Babe."

I jump, feeling Ryan's finger run down my cheek. I turned slowly to look, finding Ryan staring at me.

"Were you saying something?"

He gives me a look.

"Hey, guys, sorry, but we have to go," Ryan says. He stands, takes his wallet from his back pocket, retrieving an American Express Gold card.

He hands the card to Bradley. "Dude, pay for dinner and don't let me see no weird charges on there."

"Let's go." He reaches out and takes my hand as I stand.

"I will talk with you later," I whisper to Tinea.

Chapter Seventeen

We walk over to the coffee shop, Rise and Grind. The young girl, Sarah—the name written on her name tag-locks dreamy eyes with Ryan. He stands behind me, brushing his front against my back.

I can't blame her. His dark blue jeans, black polo shirt with a pair of Jordans, plus those eyes, and chiseled jaw line. I get it.

I order a macchiato, while Ryan gets an espresso. I spot a table in the corner by the window for two. He pulls out my chair.

I take a sip of my coffee, looking around. I spot a fountain with water spewing from the mouth of an angel.

Odd but majestic.

"Are you mad at me?" He squares his shoulders.

I look at him over my cup of coffee. "What do you think?"

"Let's not play twenty questions."

"Allllrrrighty then." I place my coffee cup on the table. "Honestly, I am feeling mixed emotions. I am mad. Saddened that you didn't tell me. Jealous that you are spending the entire summer with her, before you leave for college. That news would have been better received coming from you. Would I still be jealous? Hell, yeah. When did you find out?"

He takes a heavy breath.

"It's something both families do every summer.

Our moms have been best friends since college."

The jigsaw pieces of the puzzle start to come together. Their moms have it all planned out. The only thing is that Ryan isn't into Madeline.

"So where does that leave us?" I sit on my trembling hands. I look at him with raised eyebrows.

"Still together. I had planned on staying with my folks for two months; then spending the rest of the summer with you, until I leave for NYU."

I sip a big gulp of coffee, thawing a little bit of the ice that crystalized over my heart at the news of Ryan being with Madeline for the summer. I slant my head, scanning his face.

"When were you going to tell me? The day you were leaving?"

He runs his hand through his hair. "No, you would have known bef-"

"School ends in two weeks. When are you leaving?"

"One week after school gets out."

I nod, letting the information absorb.

"Wow!"

I take off, throwing my cup in the bin by the door. A hand pushes open the door.

"I'm sorry. Baby, I would have told you by the weekend."

"Yeah, right, and I'm Naomi Campbell."

I stomp down the sidewalk.

He swings my shoulder around, bringing me to halt.

"Hold on!" He grits his teeth. "I love you, Simone." He points to my chest. "You. No one else."

I want to believe him, I do. I just don't trust that he will take care of my heart.

"Can you please just take me home?"

He lets out a hard breath and bends forward as he

grabs his hair.

He looks up at me. "I'm not losing you over this. I'm sorry I didn't say anything sooner."

I nod. "Okay, let's just go."

Sitting in the car, I gaze straight ahead, lost in my thoughts, unaware of the passing streets.

Ryan touches my shoulder. "We're here."

At the sound of his voice, I turn and look into his eyes. I look around, and to my surprise, we are sitting in the guest parking spot at my apartment complex.

When did we get here?

"Well, goodnight," I say, reaching to open the door.

"Sim, wait." He holds on to my shoulder.

I casually turn my head, giving him a weary smile.

He caresses my cheek with his index finger.

I close my eyes. Every time he touches me, warmth spreads through me. It makes it harder to stay mad at him long.

"You are so freaking beautiful, and such a caring, loving, compassionate person. I can't handle you being mad with me."

I open my eyes, studying his face. The normal glow that shines from his emerald eyes are dim; remorse shines in them.

"I was wrong for not telling you. I should have told you long ago. Please forgive me," he says as he swipes his index finger down my face to my bottom lip.

"Please." He leans over the console and gently kisses my lips.

"Forgive me." Kiss.

"Please forgive me." Kiss.

"Will you?" Kiss. Kiss. Kiss. Kiss.

I shake my head yes. I surrender.

He cups my face between his hands and kisses me

92

as if he has been through a drought and I am his water source.

My body melts into his.

I sit on the red, plastic chair on the patio transfixed in the new Sweet Valley High book. The bright rays of the sun beams down, raining muggy heat like it's hell.

Sweat runs down my forehead, the bridge of my nose, my cheeks, down my neck, adding to my soggy tank top.

I close my eyes, fanning myself with my book. Images of a summer lost reflects off my eyelids. Ryan and I at the beach, traveling to Tampa, the haunted house at Saint Augustine, Disneyland, the NSYNC or Backstreet Boys concerts.

I reach down, taking the sweat drenched can of Sprite off the ground, rubbing it on my neck to alleviate some of the heat.

I need to take a cold shower. It's hot as hell out here.

I walk into the wall, my eyes fixated on the novel. "Crap." I throw the book on my bed, then jump into the shower.

Cold water is the best luxury on Earth today. The feel of the water running down my face to my toes, washing away the icky feeling of the afternoon heat is heaven.

Comfortable in another white tank top and shorts, I lay on the couch watching Lifetime. My phone rings. I quickly dig through the crease of the couch, hoping it's Ryan calling.

I smile.

"Hi."

"Hey, baby. How's your day going?"

"It's hot. How is yours?"

He laughs. "Okay. Missing you though."

"I miss you too. Where are you now?"

It's been a month since Ryan left with his family on their European summer vacation. Time ticked by slowly. Adding to my loneliness, Tinea left for Texas with her family two weeks ago.

I was excited when Tinea said that her parents invited me along for the journey, but Mom shut that down.

"Still Italy for three more days, then France."

"Send me pics."

"Will do, I have to go, babe. Talk with you soon." He rushes off the phone.

I call Ryan a few times, but we always seem to miss each other; time difference and all. I miss hearing his velvet voice. We text each other, and I get a few pics of the sights he saw in Italy; from the Colosseum, St. Peter's Basilica, Trexi Fountain, Piazza Navona, and the Sistine Chapel.

One day I will see that in person.

I wake in bed to the tapping of raindrops outside my window. I enjoy days like this; the soothing rhythm of the raindrops. It beats the scolding Florida summer heat.

A chime interrupts my solace. I reach for my phone off the carpeted floor. I lie back under my blanket, scrolling through the beautiful images Ryan has sent. The Louvre Museum, Cathedral Notre-Dame, Eiffel Tower …

I gasp.

Tears spring from my eyes. My fears materialized. I'm staring at a picture of Ryan kissing Madeline in front of the Eiffel Tower.

That picture is the final jigsaw piece I need to complete the puzzle. It builds the story of the image of them together: married, house on the intercostal, blue-and-green-eyed babies.

The final jigsaw piece that replaces the chipped pieces of crystal back around my heart.

I copy the picture, replying to Ryan.

RI: See you're having a great time in France. WE ARE DONE!!!

Chapter Eighteen

A month and a half ago, I would have never thought that this is where I would be. Surrounded by boxes in a strange room, in a strange city, in a strange state.

It took Mom, me, and Uncle Sam eleven hours to get to Raleigh, North Carolina. It all happened so fast.

My eyes wander over to the window, watching the sunset. I huff, sitting down on the bed, unpacking forgotten.

Ryan and I have been together for six months. I considered our relationship to be good. I speculate that it was a normal relationship. It's the only relationship I have had, it's the only reference I have. We have fought once, and that lasted only a few hours.

Ryan has the ability to chip away at the block around my heart. With him, I feel free, reckless, wanted. He was my hope of being loved.

I lay in bed with a shadow that lingers in the bottom of my mind. No appetite, lying in an unforgiving pain.

Tears wash down my face into my mouth. My tongue is saturated with the salty release of my heartbreak.

It's been two days since my world upended.

No call.

No text.

No messenger pigeon.

Nothing.

I didn't expect the silence. He said he loved me. I expected him to fight for us.

The pain and the urge to cry were fleeting as the days passed.

"Mija."

I turn toward my mom. She rests her forehead on the door frame. Worry laces her face.

Mom came home and found me curled up in a fetal position the afternoon I received the photo. I told her about the photography and that I didn't want to talk about it. She came onto the bed and wrapped her arms around me.

"You want a slice of pizza or some of the leftover food?"

I shake my head no.

"Okay, baby. I have to go and will be home by 5 today."

"Okay." The rasp in my voice is an unfamiliar sound.

I turn away from the door, back to the morning sunlight. A foul odor assaults my nose.

What the heck is that?

I lift my arm, whiff my arm pits. *Damn, you stink.*

I drag myself off the bed and take a quick shower.

An angry sound comes from my stomach with a not-so-subtle sharp pain. My stomach growls again in furry. I cover my stomach with my hand.

I stroll into the kitchen, taking the leftover Ropa Vieja from the fridge.

I open the container, my stomach rumbling as the

spice and herbs invades my nose. I serve a small portion, not wanting to get sick from overeating, and warm it in the microwave.

My mouth waters as I bring the fork full of rice and shredded beef to my mouth. I close my eyes, savoring the peppers and onions. My tastebuds dance, enjoying the array of flavors. My stomach rejoices.

I yawn, exhaustion hitting me like a dump truck.

It's the first restful sleep I have had in days.

3:30 pm. I awake refreshed. I walk to the living room, retrieving my unfinished novel from the coffee table.

BAM!

BAM!

BAM!

I jolt.

Is that the police?

I drop the book back on the coffee table and walk to the door. I open the door.

"WHAT THE FUCK DID YOU SEND ME?" Ryan yells, standing in the hallway.

I look out to see if his voice drew any of my neighbors' attention.

"Don't yell at me."

He pushes by me into the living room.

I close the door, then brace myself against the wall.

He walks around the living room like a caged animal.

"We are done." He drags his hands down his face. "You send me crap like that."

I fold my arms. "We are done."

"You just assume things, you—"

"I can't assume what I saw," I scream. "You were kissing her."

"I didn't kiss her. She kissed me. I was caught off guard. I pushed her away."

I laugh, throwing my hands up.

"Right, okay. She kissed you. Why didn't you call and tell me when you got my text? How did the pic get on your phone? How did you send it to me?" I counter pacing back and forth.

"She must have had someone ta—"

I hold my hand up. "Stop. I don't want to even know." I shake my head. "I love you. I really love you; I have never felt this way about anyone. Loving you just seems too hard. She is a battle that I will lose. It's best for us to part when the battle scars aren't life threatening."

His face turns red and hardens. He balls his fist.

"I love you, Simone. Unconditionally. It will always be you. I am not him."

My lips quiver, my eyes grow heavy with tears. I can't believe he would bring up my dad. I told him that stuff not for it to be used against me. I can't believe he went there. I shake my head. I open the front door wide.

"Goodbye."

He looks at me with longing and lost. He walks toward the door, stops, and places a kiss on my lips.

"I love you," he whispers.

The days slowly crawl by; night and day easily intertwine. Tinea calls me constantly, filling me in on her daily routine, which includes her summer fling, Mark. Days spent at the beach or pool. Nights filled with wanton desires.

Her distractions help me to get through most of the day without much thoughts of him. As hard as I have tried to forget it, my love for Ryan remains. He seized my beating heart. I pray for its return one day.

Mom finds me stretched out on the couch, staring at the ceiling, invaded by the thoughts flickering in my mind.

She bends, kisses me on the forehead, and looks at me directly in the eyes. "Each day will get easier. The tears will stop. The feeling of your heart shattering will cease. You're young, and you will love again."

I smile, hoping she is right. Hoping I will be able to dream in technicolor again.

The weeks go by, and summer vacation is coming to an end. Tinea will be back on Friday, only three more days until I can see my best friend. Two weeks away from my senior year.

The sound of boisterous laughter comes from the living room. Walking down the hall, I find Uncle Sam and Mom engaged in a lively discussion.

"Hey, Uncle Sam."

"Hey, chica. Come sit right here." He pats the left couch cushion.

I plop down beside him. "What's up?"

"Your mom and I have something to talk with you about."

"Okay." I look from side to side at Mom and Uncle Sam.

"I have been offered a great job opportunity in North Carolina. Your mom and I have been talking, and we both agreed that this would be a great move for all of us."

Silence.

I squint my eyes, not quite comprehending the words that just came out of his mouth. School starts in two weeks. This is my senior year.

My senior year.

I swallow and looked at Uncle Sam.

"Well, I am happy about … hmmm … the opportunity that you have gotten. It's good and all, but I don't know how Mom and I got roped into moving."

"Simone." Mom leaves the chair, walks over and sits next to me on the brown couch, taking my hand into hers. "Mija, Sam is the only relative we have in Florida. When he leaves, it will just be you and me. We lean on each for support a lot. You know he made the move to Florida after Jim left. Sam gave up his life in New York to be here with us. Now he has this great opportunity, and I believe it's our time to be there for him."

"I understand. Trust me I do." I turn to look at Uncle Sam. "I appreciate all that you have done. Always jumping in whenever Mom wasn't able to … but this is my senior year," I stress. "It's one year." I turn back to Mom. "Why can't we stay here until the end of senior year and then we relocate?"

"Simone, I am sorry, but I have already made the decision."

"What!" I jump off the couch. "You weren't asking me; you are telling me." I point to myself. "I don't have a say?"

"No, you don't," she says flatly.

"School starts in two weeks. Tinea gets back on Friday."

"And we will be leaving next weekend."

"What about your job?" I point at Mom.

"I already gave the Mulligans my two weeks' notice."

"This is unbelievable. I can't believe you are doing this to me," I yell.

Mom shrugs. "It's for the best. You don't see it now, but it is."

"AHHHHHHH!" I scream, turn, and storm off to my room. I slam my door, the loud noise cracking in the air.

My protest, pleading, and whining are ignored. Tinea and I even come up with the brilliant idea of me living with her for the year. I approach Mom with the idea.

"No! Did you start packing yet?" Mom replies.

"Not yet," I sulk.

Tinea spends the final week at my home. We pack, we laugh, we cry at memories we shared. We have been best friends since the fourth grade.

We hold on to each other and bawl the day of the move. We will see each other in November; Tinea's parents agreed that she could visit for Thanksgiving. Then we'll be together again next fall at Baker University.

I didn't think it would truly end this way for Ryan and me. At least I hoped that over time we would be able to be friends.

The move is the icing on the cake. I will never see Ryan Mulligan again.

Chapter Nineteen

PRESENT

Four years have passed since I last laid eyes on Ryan. Whispers of him often torment my mind with questions, driving me to the brink of insanity. Does he ever think of me? Is he dating Madeline? Is he happy? Does he look like the image I have embedded in my brain? Does he still love me? Does he compare me to the girls that he dates?

I have compared him to every guy I have dated. First date with Rick, he didn't open the car door, the door to the restaurant, or pull out my chair; Ryan would have done that. Sheldon's kiss was a wet mess, too much teeth; Ryan kisses were slow and certain, filled with passion that always ignited.

Yes, it was unfair, but …

My heart rate accelerates with the anticipation, the fear of tonight. I should be excited; it's my best friend's twenty-first birthday.

Tinea's parents went all out, shutting down Syders, the most popular club in the city. Celebrities venture to Syders nightly. You can stand in the line all day, if you are not on the list, you are not getting in. I can't fathom the price tag for tonight's shindig. Only the best for my girl.

Most people see the snob, take-no-prisoners bitch. My bestie is the girl who knows when to push me and when to pull back. The person I laugh most with. The person who always has my back no matter if I am wrong, then will tell me I was wrong to the side. The person that treated me more than a friend but as a sister. She is a driven, caring, but a fierce woman.

Junior year she made the decision that Baker was not the right choice and dropped out. Her family owns a real estate company in Florida and Texas; she wanted to sell properties instead. College wasn't going to help her.

Her dad was livid. They argued. She won. She moved out of the Beta Phi house and rented a small apartment in Tribeca. Tinea enrolled in an education course in real estate, passed the New York real estate exam, got her license, and hasn't looked back.

Her first sale is a 2500-square feet three bedroom, three bathroom apartment I now reside in. Her first client, her dad.

I look in the full-length mirror leaning in the corner bedroom wall. The black, square neck bandage dress hugs my hips, the red Louboutin's—a Christmas gift from Tinea—helps to accentuate my ass. Big, loose curls in my hair, barely there makeup on my face—bb cream, mascara, and red lips.

Damn, I would drool over me.

Music blasts through the wall mounted sound bar. Tinea opens a bottle of Don Perignon. The cork flies across the kitchen.

"Let's get this party started, bitches!"

"Yeah, I am getting wasted tonight." Jackie downs the champagne.

Jackie the crazy Jamaican became my roommate freshman year after Tinea decided to pledge Beta Phi. She has some frayed edges, she's quick to argue, but quick to love. Each guy she dates is going to be her husband, not jokingly. Been through a lot of drinking heartbreaks. Her mouth is not her own, her honesty is brutal. It cuts deep. She enjoys life, loves to laugh, eat, and dance.

She blends perfectly with us. A perfect balance of hard and soft.

We arrive at Spyders at 10:30 p.m. The black and red decor accentuated by white lights dance to the rhythm of the music across the club. Black, gothic chandeliers hang from the ceiling.

I like this, this is sexy.

Each glass of champagne and tequila is a good coping mechanism. My fear of seeing Ryan vanishes. I will make him eat his heart out.

My eyes wander toward the front door intermittently, waiting for him to arrive. As the clock ticks closer to midnight, my heart slowly deflates.

I guess he didn't want to see me again.

"What's that look for?" Tinea asks.

"Nothing." I smile, a shadow of sadness in my eyes.

"Don't give me your fake smile."

"Happy birthday, girl!" Paul yells above the sound of the music. "The big twenty-one. Time for another shot."

He passes a shot of tequila to Tinea, Jackie, and me. "One, two, three."

I throw my head back, the tequila slithers down my throat. I bite into a wedge of lime.

"I need some water. I'm not going to be able to keep up without it." I scrunch my face from the tartness of the lime.

The group laughs.

"You're such a lightweight," Paul says.

I extend my middle finger walking out of VIP.

Walking toward the bar, I stop as Sean bumps into me.

"I have been looking for you. When are you going to dance with me?"

I step back. Sean's breath reeks of alcohol. "Soon, big boy." I pat him on his chest and step around.

Nearing the bar, I spot a group of guys laughing in loud conversations with three girls; one girl I recognize from my marketing class.

The guy in the black, leather jacket turns around. Intense green eyes entrap me.

"Who the hell is he?" I hear Paul's voice at the right of me.

"Bomboclat, him yummy." Jackie to the left.

"Carajo (fuck me sideways)," I whisper, frozen.

It's Ryan.

Chapter Twenty

My eyes grow to saucers. He looks good, better than the images my mind stored. I can tell that his body is more defined, shoulders a tad bit boarder and muscled. I bet his six pack is now a ripped eight pack. His hair is disheveled. It works.

I want to launch myself at him. My body sizzles, longing for his touch. This was not the reaction I was expecting to have.

His eyes never leave mine. He sees all the emotions that are moving through me. I feel naked standing here.

Mariah Carey's "Without You" blares around the club. The words wrap tightly and squeezed my heart. I fight against the tears that are threatening to fall.

How the hell did the DJ go from playing Snoop Dog to this? Why is the universe messing with me?

"You know what, screw the water. Let's get some more shots." I turn, walking back to VIP room.

I fill the shot glass with Don Julio tequila, downing it like water. I reach for the bottle of tequila again.

Tinea grabs the bottle from my hand. "Slow down, Simone. You know you can't hang with the big boys," she chides. "I am not taking care of you tonight if you get wasted. Come here." We walk to the railing. "You see that fine, walking, sex-on-a-stick standing next to Ryan?"

I stare at Ryan.

"He's going to put the icing on my cake tonight."

I glance at the guy, white shirt, sleeve rolled up to his elbow.

The guy waves to Tinea. She giggles, beckons him to come up.

The guy turns around and talks with Ryan.

Ryan glances up at us, and nods his head. Our eyes collide.

I quickly look away; l lean against the railing.

"Girrrlll, you know the fine ass in the black jacket?" Paul asks.

I nod. "That's Ryan."

"That's Ryan!!! He is hot," Jackie screeches. "You stupid for breaking up with him."

I squint my eyes as I looked at Jackie. "He kissed another girl."

"And …" She holds her hands up. "He left his family in Europe, just to assure you that there was nothing between him and the girl. You dumb. I would have fucked his brains out."

Paul nods in agreement with Jackie. "She's right."

Of course, she would have. I roll my eyes. I look over the balcony and catch Ryan staring at me. His look says I am in so much trouble.

I drag Paul by his arm. "Let's go downstairs and dance."

I let the music take over my body, possessed by the rhythm and the bass. I gyrate, shaking all my body parts. I grind on Paul, my head on his chest, my eyes closed, imagining that it's Ryan instead.

The song ends. I look at Ryan, his hands wrapped tightly around the waist of another girl. A sharp pain pinches my chest.

"I'm going to the restroom," I sniffle.

I stare at myself in the bathroom mirror, trying to

will myself to approach him.

You can walk right up to him. You can do it. Don't be a pussy. It's just Ryan. You can do this, Simone. You got this, girl.

A loud breath escapes me. I stand tall, straighten my shoulders, and exit the bathroom.

After a quick scan of the room, I find him still at the bar. I look for the blonde upon my approach; she's nowhere in sight.

I stare into his eyes. "Hi." I smile.

"Hi," the guy to the left of him replies.

I glance at the stranger, smile and return his greetings. Ryan stands still, looking at me, no reply.

"What's your name?" the stranger asks, a curve to his lips.

"Simone." I slant my head.

Still not a word from Ryan.

"You are beautiful."

"Thanks." I fidget with my fingers. I look back at Ryan; silence drifts between us.

"Ryan, how have you been?"

"Dude, I am going to stop hanging around you. All these fine ass girls only want to talk with you for some reason. Baby, I'm way better," the stranger with the blue shirt declares.

"Yeah …" I shake my head. Looking back to Ryan, he continues to stare at me as if I'm insignificant.

I nod, understanding.

"Okay." I roll my eyes and walk to the other side of the bar.

It hurts. I'm humiliated. A new wound, a new scar added. He was cold. I went to him, and he rejected me. He's added a new wound for me to shed.

I yell to get the bartender's attention. I order a

tequila shot and a strawberry margarita. A single tear slides down my face. I flick it away with my index finger.

Don't let him see you cry.

I want to run and hide in my safe place. Tinea's upset and disappointed face is something I want to avoid. I may be hurt, but this night isn't about me.

I down the tequila and put the margarita to my mouth.

I smell him, before I feel him. He presses his front to my back.

"I'm sorry," he whispers in my ear.

"It's fine, excuse me." I begin to move around him. I stumble.

He catches me around the waist.

"You okay?"

"I'm fine." I bat his hand away from my waist. "Let go."

He ignores my plea. "How many shots have you had?"

"Six … nine … I don't know." Twinkling lights dance in my eyes.

"You're drunk," he snaps.

"First for everything. Another first because of you." I laugh.

"Hold on to me, we need to get some water and food in your system."

I drink both bottles of water and eat half of a cheeseburger. I sit still, waiting for the burger to absorb some of the liquor.

"You okay, girly?" Tinea asks.

"I'm feeling a little better."

"He'll always take care of you." She winks. She blushes as she looks to the guy she has been with for half of the night.

"I'm going home with Craig tonight," she whispers.

"Yeah. Good for you. Live it up." I nod.

"You going to be okay?"

"I am. I am going to head out in a little. You okay with that?"

"Yeah, girl, I going to maul that stud."

I place a kiss on her cheek. "Love you. Best birthday party ever!"

"Thanks."

It's time to leave. I walk around the VIP room, saying goodbye to her family and our friends. I walk to where Ryan and Craig stand talking.

"Hey, Ryan. I want to tell you thanks for earlier."

"Anytime." He smiles.

"It was nice seeing you again."

"You leaving?"

"Yeah, I'm heading out."

"Dude, I will see you later," Ryan says to Craig.

"I will head out with you," he says as he takes my hand.

Chapter Twenty-One

I wake up to my head thumping like a drum being played by Chris Shaw of Savage, my favorite alternative music band.

"Gahhh ..."

The bright sunlight pours into the room. I quickly close my eyes, slowly opening them a second time. I look around the room, no sign of familiarity. My heart is thundering. Masculine, espresso furnishings surround me.

To my left, a glass of orange juice and two Advil lay on the night stand.

That's nice. I hope someone isn't trying to drug me.

I place the pills on my tongue, guzzle the orange juice, swallowing my cure to this pounding in my head.

Did I have a one-night stand? Oh gosh ... please don't be naked, please don't be naked.

I peep under the covers to find that I am wearing a blue t-shirt sans dress. I creep out of the room in search of answers to where I am.

I stop at the sight of the man standing on the patio shirtless, in running shorts, barefoot. I know it's Ryan. His back muscles flex as if he's aware of my presence. I admire how sculpted his form is, not bulky, defined. His waist tapers into his shorts; a gush of moisture soaks my thong.

"Hey, sleepy head." He catches me drooling. "Finally, up."

I place my finger over my lips. "Sssshhhh …
coffee."

He laughs. "Do you still like it with milk and sugar?"

"Milk and sugar."

I walk out to the patio and lounge onto the red
chaise while he makes coffee. The view is
magnificent—lush, green trees—but I am too
hungover to move and enjoy the view.

Gray clouds reign the morning sky, bringing a cold
bite with the breeze. I close my eyes and drift off.

Electricity zaps through me at the gentle rub of
Ryan's hand across my face. I peek up at him. Heaven,
Ryan serving me coffee shirtless. As appealing as the
coffee is, licking or kissing up and down his chest
appeals to me more.

I clear my throat. "Do you have a syringe?"

"For?" His eyes sparkle with humor.

"Quicker way to consume it without having to move
any part of me." I take the cup from his hands.

I shrink at the boisterous laughter.

"I will never get wasted again." I sip the
deliciousness. The warmth creates a tingling sensation.

He sits on the chaise across from me, watching me.
I shift, uncomfortable and excited by his perusal. I can
see a thunderstorm brewing in his eyes.

I don't understand why he brought me here. Did he
feel the need to take care of me?

I glance at him over the coffee cup.

"How did I get here?"

He scrunches up his face. "You don't remember?"

"I recall us leaving the club. The array of stars
glistening in front of my eyes. We were walking down
the street … that's it."

"More like I was carrying you down the street. You

fainted. I got us a cab back to my place since I don't know where you live or how we would have gotten in." He runs his hand through his already disheveled hair. "I carried you upstairs to the spare bedroom. You stripped out of your dress, complaining that you couldn't sleep in it. I grabbed you one of my shirts and tucked you in bed."

Oh. He saw me in nothing but a string for a thong.

"Thanks for taking care of me."

"I would have it no other way."

I can see that this conversation is heading for somewhere that I am not ready for yet. I walk back into his apartment, leaving him sitting out on the patio.

It's time for you to leave, Simone.

I go back in the room and find my dress folded on the bedroom bench.

"Are you running?" My body trembles at the sound of his voice.

I swallow, turning to see him standing in the doorway. His previously shirtless top is now covered in a polo shirt. He surveys my body from top to bottom. I smell his hunger and the same lust that escapes from my pores.

I run my tongue across my lips. "I'm not running." The breathy sound of my voice echoes.

He crosses his arms across his chest. "Then what are you doing?"

That voice. How I missed hearing it. "I am going home. I just feel really exhausted."

Bitch, you lying. You running.

He steps forward, I step backward. We play this game until I am back against the bed.

A flirtatious smile comes over his face. I put my hands on his chest, halting his advance. I lick my lips

114

at the feel of his eight pack through his shirt.

God why are you doing this to me?

"I know you feel it, Simone. Stop running."

I swallow. He lowers his head to mine. My insides rejoice, imagining his mouth on mine.

We stall at the sound of the doorbell.

"The door," I quickly point out.

"Don't move," he growls as he leaves.

What are you doing, Simone? Yes, you can feel the chemistry, but can you stand another heartbreak? This is the one guy you can't hide from. It's best to leave.

I come around the corner and see Ryan's body blocking the partially opened door.

I stand behind him and rise to my tip toes to peak over his shoulder. A girl with a model's physique, strawberry blonde hair cut in a sharp bob, and face made-up to perfection stands on the other side.

"Who the fuck is this, Ryan?" she hisses.

I know I looked great last night, but this morning is a different story. My hair could use a brush, and I know my makeup is jacked. I felt plain compared to her dressed in a white tank, black skinny jeans, beige wool coat, and red ankle boots.

She has legs for days. I can't compete with her.

"Monica, I need you to leave. This is not a good time," he says slowly.

"Is this why I couldn't see you last night!?" She looks at me with disgust.

If looks could kill, with the way she is looking at me, I could turn to cinder. You can have him. This is why it's smart to walk away.

"Could you move, Ryan? I've got stuff to do."

"Monica, we will speak later," he says briskly, slamming the door in Monica's face.

"Why did you close the door? I told you I have to go." I say, standing my ground.

"I can't lose you again."

His lips brush mine.

Chapter Twenty-Two

He abruptly lifts and spins me. I gasp as my back collides with the door. His mouth smashes mine. It is rough, aggressive, and sensual. It's not the soft and gentle kisses my memory stored. The intensity scares me.

I am scared of what this kiss means. I am scared not to read too much into it. I am scared. I can feel the fears that run through my mind. The fears that takes my troubled memories, uses them to ravage my confidence; that I am wanted, that I am loved, that I am enough.

He kisses my necking. I crumble. It only takes a few touches of his sexual lips, to take my mind away from my inner tormentor.

Myself.

A wave of pleasure crashes through my body.

Oh God!

I melt into his arms.

"Wait. Wait." I push against his chest.

He pauses, his head on mine.

"For what?" he asks, his voice low and husky.

The words in my head remain stagnant.

He lets out a heavy breath. "I have thought about you every day since you chased me away. Not being able to talk, touch, or see you did something to me. I planned on giving you space for a while. My mom bitched and complained about me being gone. Dad called, and I went back."

I look up into his eyes. Stupefied, not expecting him to feel this way. I'm not the only one that mourned the loss of us.

I walk and sit on his loveseat with my hand on my cheeks.

"I was a seventeen-year-old, head over heels in love with a guy. Who happened to also be the son of my mother's employer. I don't know what happened, one minute I am elated, over the moon. The next I'm in hell. Besides my father, you are the only other person that has the power to annihilate me. I'm scared I am not good enough. I'm not from the right family. What your family thinks matters to you. In the long run, you are going to leave me just like he did."

I can't believe I'm telling him this.

He kneels in front of me, placing his hands on my thighs. I flinch when his thumb wipes the tear from my eye.

I missed gazing into his rich, forest green eyes.

"Sim, baby. I make the decisions for my life. Not my mom, not my dad, ME. I didn't find out that your mom left until we came back from Europe. I refused to believe she had quit. Rose had been with us for years. I went by your apartment, banging on the door until your noisy neighbor came out. She told me you guys had moved."

"I'm sorry, I pushed you away. I'm sorry I didn't believe you about the kiss." The vessel opens, tears run down my cheeks. He holds me in his arms until the vessel closes.

"I need to head home."

"Okay, I will take you."

A whirlwind of emotions assaults me; the possibility

118

of us, sadness, regret, and fear. I stand by the door as he goes to retrieve his keys. It's a solemn elevator ride to the garage. We had both revealed a lot.

I follow him until he opens the passenger door to a matte black Range Rover. He asks for my address as we leave the garage.

Thick tension consumes the car. We still have not defined what happens from here.

"Do you remember the time I got gum in your hair?" He laughs, breaking the tension.

"Yeah, jerk." I shove his shoulder.

We sit in the car, laughing, reminiscing about the past. Beside Tinea, he's the one person that I have shared the most with. I can be myself around him, I don't have to worry about being awkward or goofy. It's so comfortable and easy to speak with him.

I look at the entrance of my apartment building, hesitant to open the door and leave.

"So … thanks for the ride. It was good seeing you again."

"I want you back. I am serious, Sim. I want you back." His voice hardens, leaving no trace of misunderstanding.

"Okay, let's start out slow." I stretch forth my hand. "Friends."

He nods and kisses the back of my hand.

"If that's all I can get for NOW, friends."

Chapter Twenty-Three

I sit on the couch, rubbing my pulsing feet. Another day working the midday shift at Bread Basket Cafe. Working twenty hours each week provides me with basic necessities: food, some clothing, and pocket money. I'm fortunate having not to think about paying rent, water, or electricity. Tinea affords me that luxury. We argued about me paying for the cable, but eventually I won. She's a great friend; I don't want her to think that I would ever take advantage of her generosity.

It's been nice reconnecting with Ryan. We try to carve out time to see each other in between classes, studying, and work. Ryan's been working at the Mulligan Group's New York office, getting acclimated to the business he will run one day. He's required to spend a couple months in each department. We meet for coffee, dinner, and sometimes he pops in to the cafe in between my break.

It is important for us to have a strong and good foundation built on our friendship. The last thing I want is to repeat our past mistakes.

I love talking with him, witnessing how our words tie together, displaying the depth of our hearts.

The chemistry between us sizzles without a touch or a word. It's constantly present.

I get lost in my mind, unable to focus. A whisper of my imagination, our bodies intertwined, his mouth wrapped around my beaded nipples—the desire and the pain of wanting constantly on my mind.

"Mini Ryan," my vibrator, has gotten more action in the past couple weeks than the past couple years I've owned it.

Tinea and Craig stroll into the kitchen laughing. The two have been practically inseparable since her birthday. Apparently, sparks flew. Then clothes flew; they have been a couple ever since.

I look at them, smiling.

I love the way he dotes on her. The constant glow that follows her because of him is a welcome sight. I can see their complete picture. I can see the happily ever after for them. I was shocked when she told me that he was the one. I have never known her as the girl that gets wrapped up in a relationship. She goes with the flow.

Ohh, how the tide has turned.

"Hey, you two."

"Hey, girl."

"I haven't seen my boy lately," Craig says, standing behind Tinea with his arms around her. He playfully bites at her ear.

"I have hardly spent any time with my girl." I point my finger in their direction. I clear my throat. "Also, if you two can keep the nightly moaning down. I do need to sleep." I toss a bag of potato chips across the living room at the pair.

Craig backs away from Tinea, shaking his head. "I need to call my boy. He ain't doing something right." He grabs his phone off the kitchen island.

"You better not," I yell at his receding back.

I wish he was doing something.

"Don't pay him any attention, Simone. What are

121

you up to tonight?" Tinea asks as she moves her eyebrows up and down.

I hold my stomach as I erupt in laughter. "I'm having dinner with Ryan at his house."

"The penthouse ... so many things can happen." She grabs a bottle of water from the fridge, then makes her way to the couch.

"Nothing will happen. We will eat and talk." I shrug.

"Yeah right. Do the nasty."

"Nooooo ... stop it."

"I have missed you, babe. We need to have a girl's day complete with the spa, popcorn, ice cream, rom-com, and wine."

"Yeah, that will be great. Let me see what my work schedule is for the next two weeks. We can set something up then."

"Definitely."

"I've got to get going. Have fun tonight; keep it down. I have an early class in the morning." I hug her and stand to go and get ready.

"I can't promise, but I'll try." She grins.

I change into a light gray, plunge neck sweater, light blue jeans, and black buckle strapped platform stiletto ankle boots. My hair is in a ponytail, no makeup, and red lip gloss. I pull out my favorite pea coat; without it, the cold weather will seep through my sweater.

I'm greeted by George, the concierge for Ryan's building. I enter the elevator, tap my keycard, and press P.

Excitement bounces through every crevice of my body. Once I'm with him, the sensation only intensifies.

The elevator opens, and there he stands in the living room looking esculent in a white shirt, dark jeans, and shoeless.

"Hey, beautiful."

"Hey." I blush.

The last time I was here was the night of Tinea's birthday party.

I purposely brush against him as I walk by to admire the floor to ceiling glass view. I suck air through my teeth; Central Park at night is stunning.

The hair on the back of my neck stands up. I glance behind me, finding him watching me.

What is going on in that brain of yours?

I saunter over to him. "So."

"So ..." he replies.

I shiver at the sound of his husky voice.

"What's on the agenda for tonight?"

"A movie. And if you're good, dinner."

I bite my index finger, squinting my eyes. "I will only get dinner if I'm good? Lucky for me I am not that hungry."

He laughs, his eyes darken. He licks his lips.

I wish I was his lips. Damn, he's sexy.

"What are we watching?" My voice sounds as if a frog got stuck in it. I cough, trying to clear my throat.

"Are you okay? You need water or something?" he asks with an emphasis on something.

I shake my head. Every nerve and cell in my body and brain is electrified. The anticipation of something more happening is thick in the air. I know that once we journey down this road, there will be no going back.

"Fast and Furious. Have you seen it?"

"No. What, no romantic comedy?" I hold my hands up.

"Hilarious, Sim." He stalks off to the living room.

I bite my lip, admiring his form as he walks away,

before following.

Oh Lord, help me.

I keep sneaking looks at him during the movie. His thigh brushes against mine. His perfectly symmetrical face, a roman nose, kissable lips. I get jealous every time women stop in their tracks to admire him.

I tighten my palms, my nails dig into my flesh, stopping me from mauling him. The air in the room is suffocating, my breathing becomes shallow. The smell of his cologne infiltrates my nostrils. The muscles in his thighs twitch.

I close my eyes. Images of his hands between my legs rubbing my clit on display. A sound escapes me.

I quickly open my eyes. *Did I just moan out loud?*

His eyes smolder. *His desires spelled out.* "Are you hungry?"

"No, I'm good." I lick my parched lips. "Are you hungry?"

His mouth captures mine. The kiss is frantic and hot. I gasp into his mouth as he pins me back on the couch.

"Hands up." He yanks my sweater above my head. I grab the bottom of his shirt and he helps me pull it over his head.

He bends down and sucks my beaded nipple through my black, lace bra. Switching from one nipple to the next. My head falls back; I moan.

He kisses between my boobs, kissing down my stomach. He unsnaps the button and unzips my jeans, dragging them down my legs.

I laugh, breathless, watching him expel himself of his pants and boxer briefs.

OH MY GOSH…

I shudder at the sight of him bare.

He pulls my legs toward him. He bends his head. I feel a swipe of his tongue on my clit.

"Ryan," I call out in ecstasy.

His tongue laps around and around my clit. I cry out. He continues to work me with his tongue. I felt the tightening of my core. He sucks on my nub. I explode, screaming his name.

He looks at me with hooded eyes.

"I am going to fuck you hard and fast this time."

He thrusts into me.

"Oh my God."

"No, it's just me."

He pounds into me relentlessly. He pulls my legs around his waist.

He growls into my ear, "I love how tight you are. No one else better have been here."

I am too inundated with the emotions flowing through me to acknowledge that statement.

He thrusts and rolls his hips. Back and forth, back and forth. He digs his fingers into my waist as he pounds.

"This feels so good," I gasp, arching my back.

He thrusts is tongue into my mouth, mimicking the strokes of his penis.

I tighten around his penis. He pounds harder and deeper.

I clamp onto his dick. "Oh yeah, oh yeah, that's it."

"Fuck," he yells. His head goes back as he cums.

His body weight falls on me.

We lay there for a while, trying to catch our breath. I run my hand through his damp hair.

He looks up and smiles. "No more just being friends."

I slowly bob my head.

I never make it back to my apartment that night or class the next day.

Chapter Twenty-Four

I lay across his chest, drained and sore from our pleasurable activities. Ryan runs his hand through my knotted hair.

"Let's shower and go grab something to eat."

"My legs are dead." I yawn. "I'm tired, just want to sleep." I burrow into his chest, and throw my left leg over his.

"Baby, we need to eat."

"Nooooo."

He extracts my leg from his. He slowly rises, shifting me to the center of the bed.

"Where are you going?" I ask, leaning on my elbow.

"Be right back." He kisses my forehead and walks into the bathroom.

I slowly drift off to the soothing sound of water running in the bathroom.

"Let's go, sleepy head." Ryan's strong arms lift me from the bed and carry my naked body into bathroom.

He places me inside the freestanding tub. I submerge myself, letting the warm water envelope me. Ryan slides into the water behind me. I recline back into his arms. Wrapped in love, safety, and warmth.

"I wish I could lay like this forever," I sigh.

"You can, nothing is stopping us."

"Life is stopping us. I have so much to catch up on playing hooky with you today."

"You loved it." He kisses my neck.

"I do love it." I haven't felt this content in a while.

"Spend tomorrow night with me," he says as he lazily draws circles along my stomach.

"Are you asking or telling me?"

"Telling you. I want you back in my bed."

I laugh. "That's not going to work. I am working the late shift tomorrow. I have to catch up on what I missed today. Professor Shark is a pain. I passed the last test but the syllabus only gets harder." I glance back at him. "That requires me to focus and not get distracted by sexy men." I kiss his lips.

"I can behave myself. Can you?" His brow raises.

"I was voted the best behaved kid from pre-k to high school." I wink.

"It's settled. I will pick you up after your shift tomorrow."

His hand disappears in the water. His finger travels slowly up and down my thigh inching closer to my sex. With his other hand, he teases my nipples.

Suddenly, he inserts one finger inside me, then added another, strumming me like a guitar.

He tweaks my breasts.

A throaty moan escapes me.

My muscles clench tightly around his fingers as he pumps in and out of me. His thumb rubs my clit, heightening my sensation.

He pumps, rubs, tweaks, and pumps and rubs and tweaks. It's sensory overload.

I grab onto the sides of the tub.

"Don't stop."

The pleasure is hallucinatory.

I throw my head back, shuddering as I detonate.

"Let's shower and get something to eat," he whispers. He carries me to the shower, takes his soap, and washes my body.

Our order of teriyaki shrimp, chicken, miso soup, and vegetable tempura arrived as the sun begins to set. My mouth waters instantly at the smell of the food.

We sit on the living room carpet, our backs leaning against the couch, containers of food between us.

"This is so good," I murmur

"Let me taste the shrimp." He places his fork into the container.

I knock his fork away. "No." I pout. "You have starved me for more than twelve hours." I place a shrimp in his mouth.

"I starved you, woman? Who kept straddling me?"

"Who didn't protest?"

He looks at me dumbfounded. "Why would I? I have a hot woman ravishing my body."

I smile and shake my head.

"I have to leave soon."

"Wow, I feel so used!" He places his hand over his heart. "You use me for sex and food."

"You're stupid." I hold my stomach, bursting in laughter at his theatrics. "I'll be back tomorrow, and I will only use you for food then."

"We'll see about that."

"You promised that I would be able to study. I also need to complete the application for the summer internship at Rhodes Agency. It's my dream to land a job there after graduation."

"You will get it."

"I hope so."

"Hey, I was thinking, why don't we head up to the Hamptons next weekend before Thanksgiving break?"

"That sounds nice, but Tinea and I planned a girls' night."

"You can invite your friends. I know Craig will be up for it. Invite Jackie and Paul. It would be nice to get away from the city for a little."

"I will talk to them and let you know."

"God, I missed you." He tugs at my hair.

"I did too, baby." I look into his eyes.

He brings our lips together.

Chapter Twenty-Five

I sit on my bed reviewing the class notes Paul and Sienna were gracious to send me for my two missed classes yesterday.

Why did it have to be today Professor Shark assigned a group project?

Luckily for me, the professor didn't assign group members. I have worked with Sienna before in previous classes on other group projects. She's organized, smart, and fun to work with. My other group members consist of Sean—the flirt, Thomas, and Allison. I have seen Thomas around. Allison is friends with Sienna; they both belong to the same sorority.

My room door slams against the wall, jolting me out of my musing.

"What the hell!" I shout, scowling at Jackie and Tinea.

"Where the hell have you been, bitch? You haven't been answering your phone. You haven't returned phone calls or text messages. You skipped your classes, and you never do that. You have been MIA for almost twenty-four hours," Jackie counts, her face in a scowl. "I was getting ready to call your mom."

I put up my hands. "Sorry. I was caught up in a different world." I glance down on my laptop, heat creeping up on face.

"Caught up in Ryan's dick," Jackie says as she throws herself across my bed.

"You are so …"

"Right, that's what I am." She laughs. "How good was it, girl? Did he put it on you?"

"Come on, guys." My face burns hot.

"Details, girl, you can't keep out on us," Tinea chimes in, draping her body over the accent chair in the corner.

"There is nothing much to say. It was great, and yes, to answer your questions, Jackie," I say, hiding the smile behind my hand.

"That's it. How big is it?" Jackie uses her finger as a measurer.

"I'm not answering that."

"You can be such a prude at times." Jackie scoffs.

"Some things I like to keep to myself."

"Things have progressed then?" Tinea asks enthusiastically.

"Yeah, it's official. That's my man." I hide my face in my pillow.

"I knew it! I knew it! You guys are meant to be. He's your happily ever after."

Happily ever after? Take one tiny step at a time.

"As entertaining as this conversation has been, I've got to kick you hussies out. I have to catch up on my class work."

"Whatever." Jackie stands from the bed, pointing at me. "I'll get the details out of you sooner or later."

"Fine. I have properties to go find for the Wallaces anyways. His wife is driving me bat shit crazy. Nothing seems to be good enough. They just increased the budget to thirteen million; my commission is going to be fat." Tinea rubs her hands together.

132

"Wait, I just remembered I have to ask you all: Would you like to go to the Hamptons next weekend?"

"Hell yeah," Jackie squeals.

Tinea ponders. "I can move some stuff around and talk with Craig."

"Okay, well let me know. HAMPTONS, baby!"

"Why do you have so many bags?" Craig groans, placing Tinea's bags in the back of Ryan's RangeRover. "It's only two days."

"A girl needs options." She beams.

"Really, babe, Simone has one bag. One!" He points at my suitcase.

"Stop whining." She pats his chest.

Tinea and I sit in the back of the SUV, look at each other, and erupt in laughter, holding our stomachs, tears flowing down our faces.

"Ha, ha, ha," Craig says, entering the car. "Dude, what they laughing so hard at?"

"Leave me out of it," Ryan says, holding up his hands.

Friday afternoon traffic is gridlock. Everyone is getting out of the city for the weekend; some people traveling to Connecticut, Hamptons, or New Jersey.

We finally hit the freeway; traffic is bumper-to-bumper but moving at a steady pace. This normal one-hour-and-forty-five-minute drive will take longer if traffic persists.

I pull out my package of Twizzlers. I offer some to the group; the guys refused. I bite my lips, and glance

133

at Ryan through the rear-view mirror, my eyes bright.

He slightly raises his eyebrows.

I look away, not wanting Ryan to see the grin creeping up on my face. I take a Twizzler from the packet.

I look back at him and place the Twizzler slowly in my mouth. I lower my eyes, wrapping my tongue around the licorice, hoping I am exuding seduction.

Ryan grins.

I pop the treat out of my mouth, drag it along my chest, and swirl it between my cleaver.

His eyes grow heavy.

I trail the sweet back up along the side of my neck, wrapped my lips around it, licking and sucking, moving it around with my tongue.

He shifts from side to side, then clears his throat.

"You're playing with fire, keep it up," he growls.

"Eyes on the road, sir."

"Don't ask for something you can't handle."

"Meh," I say, waving him off.

I open my mouth and take a big bite of the Twizzler, slowly savoring the sweet treat, then swallow. I raise my brows.

"Ouch." He winces.

"What have you done to my friend, Ryan?" Tinea asks, her voice bubbly. "I mean, you turned her out."

"Shut it." I shove her.

Everyone erupts in laughter.

Night falls and the stars shine like snowflakes. We pull onto a graveled road, the property shrouded by trees.

"Babe, here are the keys. The alarm code is 825902. It's on the left side. We'll get the stuff from the car."

Arm in arm, Tinea and I walk into the home. We

find a light switch to the right of the alarm panel.

"Wow," we say in unison.

The house is indeed the Mulligans'. An open floor plan, a double living room, each having a wood burning fireplace. Wood flooring throughout (Walnut, per Tinea).

We turn on the kitchen lights. The eat-in kitchen is stunning. All top-of-the-line appliances. Everything is bathed in white and silver. Tinea runs her hand along the marble countertop and whistles. There are mahogany framed glass doors leading to a resort pool, spa, pool house, and a pergola to the right.

Outside brightens, giving a magnificent view of the surroundings. There is a built-in pizza oven, dining area, fireplace and barbeque pit. Perfect for tomorrow's pool activities.

"This is all Ryan's mom. She got taste."

"We haven't even seen the full house yet," I whisper.

I yelp. I'm tossed over Ryan's shoulder.

"Put me down."

"All that shit you were doing in the car. Time to pay the piper, baby."

He carries me up a curved staircase. He closes the door, and places me in front of him.

"Let's see what that beautiful mouth of yours can do," he whispers, then bites my ear.

I kneel on the floor. I looked up at him under my lashes. Our eyes are fixed on each other.

I timidly pull his sweatpants down. His cock salutes me.

Hmm. No boxer briefs.

My breathing accelerates. I have read about it in all these romance novels, but I have never given someone a blow job. Again, Ryan will be my first.

I run my tongue up and down his cock.

He moans.

I flatten my tongue, open my mouth, and take him inch by inch.

Paul and Jackie arrive after eleven the next day. Jackie, Tinea and I grab glasses of margarita's and lay out by the pool. Meanwhile, the guys go to the grocery store to get items for tonight's feast.

It's forty-nine degrees today, the freezing cold contradicted by the sparkling sun, creating a slight chill. I'm dressed more for comfort than necessity in a black, light sweater and leggings.

"I don't know how you bitches do it, but it is cold out here. I'm going inside." Jackie shivers and runs inside.

"Such a weakling," Tinea yells.

We decide to join her in the kitchen.

"What are you guys doing for the holidays?" I ask.

"I'm going home with Craig." Tinea face flames.

"Really, now?" Jackie nudges her. "I'm heading to Chicago to hang with some family. Where you and Ryan going?"

"Who says we are going somewhere together?"

Jackie sucks her teeth. "Do I have stupid written across my forehead?"

"Sometimes," I snicker. "I'm joking. We are going to visit Mom. She hasn't seen him in years. She's doesn't know he's coming." I bite my fingernail.

"Did she not like him?" Jackie looks puzzled.

"No, she loves him. He's like her son. The situation was just uncomfortable for her. She's going to enjoy it."

We discuss our plans for Christmas. I'm not exactly looking forward to it. Ryan wants me to spend Christmas with him in Florida. Just the thought of it causes my body to quake.

"Did you finish your Econ project yet?" Tinea questions me.

"Yeah." I contemplate if I should tell them.

"Sean kissed me," I blurt out.

"What!?" Tinea screeches.

"Are you serious!?" Jackie's eyes widen.

"Who the fuck kissed who!?" a voice rumbles.

The air in my lungs tightens. I turn, looking at the entrance of the kitchen; there stands Ryan with groceries in hand, Craig and Paul behind him.

His jaw clenches and nostrils flare.

Chapter Twenty-Six

His eyes are raw with pain. It's a sharp point digging into my ribs. He throws the grocery bags on thecounter and storms out of the kitchen.

I hang my head. A soft panic grows inside me. How am I going to handle this?

"You going to go deal with that?" Craig asks.

I nod.

Shoulders hunched; I watch as my feet take each step up the stairs. My mind desperately searches for the right words to say to him.

I find him seated on the bed, his head hung, with his hands tugging on his hair.

"Ryan?" I whisper, timidly approaching him. "Baby."

His head snaps up. He stares at me. His eyes hold no warmth, they're so cold and detached. It chills me. I look away, looking everywhere but him.

"When did this kiss happen?" The baritone of his voice vibrates through my bones.

I fidget with my hands. "Hmmm ... Thursday night after the group met."

"You kissed him?"

"What? No!" I vigorously shake my head. "Hell no, I didn't kiss him. He kissed me out of nowhere. He asked to go to coffee. I told him that we would have to do it another time. He seemed okay, then he kissed me. I pushed him off, asked him what was he doing. I told him I have a boyfriend. He doesn't believe that you exist. I told him that you did and nothing could happen between me and him. I love you," I ramble.

"Ha. I should just trust and believe that?"

My mouth drops open. "I've never given you a reason not to trust me." Fear bubbles in my gut.

"Why didn't you tell me? If I hadn't overheard you talking to your friends, would you have told me?" He fists his hand until it turns white. He scans my face, waiting for my reply.

Silence hangs suspended in the air. My mouth refuses to open. I don't want to lie, and I'm too afraid of the outcome if I tell the truth.

He stands, finger pointing as he prowls toward me. "Isn't this shit ironic? You broke up with me after Madeline kissed me. You remember that shit?"

I swallow, suppressing the fear brewing within me. I stand firm, eyes meeting his. I did nothing wrong.

Neither did he back then.

"You weren't planning on telling me!"

"I don't know." That's my honest reply. I have been conflicted about what to do. My plan was to get advice from the girls.

He shakes his head. "You're unbelievable."

"I'm sorry. I never wanted this to happen. I'm horrified that it did. I love you, Ryan. You, and only you."

I raise my hand, slowly wrapping it around his neck. I lay my head over his heart. His heartbeat echoes in my ears. The erratic pounding gradually decreases to a steady thump.

He lifts my head from his chest and gazes into my hazel eyes.

"I love you."

139

"I love you too."

We spend the rest of the afternoon cocooned into each other.

We leave the Hamptons with one resolve. We will not hide things from each other. We must trust in the love and foundation of our relationship.

The week leading up to Thanksgiving flies by. We squeeze in time for our relationship in between classes and work. We race through La Guardia, intent on not missing our flight, not willing to spend twelve hours in the car driving.

I marvel at the surrounding beauty from inside our cab. Unlike Florida, autumn in North Carolina is utterly majestic. You can always tell when summer has ended. The leaves covering the trees are freckled with red, yellow, and orange. Then comes a rustling from the wind, and a colorful rain of leaves flutter to the earth.

My mom stands at the doorway, mouth open in shock at the sight of Ryan. I was vague when I told her about a friend that would be accompanying me for Thanksgiving. Mom isn't one for surprises, but this one I was sure she would love.

"Ryan!" She smiles, but the smile doesn't reach her eyes.

That's weird.

Shock is written all over her face.

I incline my head, studying my mom's reaction.

"What are you doing here?" she asks.

140

He puts his arms around my waist, then places a kiss on my cheek. "Here to enjoy Thanksgiving with you and my favorite girl."

She's taken aback by his actions and declaration.

"Your favorite girl!?" Her brows raise.

"Babe, you haven't told her?"

"No, I haven't. I wanted to surprise you, Mom. Surprise." I throw my arms out, a small smile playing upon my lips.

"Surprised I am. Boy, come give me a hug." She stretches out her arms and welcomes Ryan. Narrow eyes greet me.

Something is off. Is she upset!?

"Come on in … let me show you to your room, Ryan."

"That's okay Rose, I can stay in Sim's room."

Mom bursts out in laughter. "I forgot how funny you are. When you marry her, then we can see about that."

A hearty laugh flows out of him as he rounds the corner. Mom gives Ryan the room across from Uncle Sam.

My eyes widen. "You're funny, Mom."

Like that is going to stop us.

The house feels quaint despite being a five-bedroom, three bathroom, 2536-square-feet rambler. The hallway walls are covered with family photographs. The living room has a fireplace that I cozy up to whenever I'm home. The paved backyard is flanked by circular beds filled with roses, tulips, and different annuals during the summer. Native trees and shrubs are thick, their roots twisted. We have come a long way from the small apartment.

Aunt Grace, her husband Frank, and my cousins

Savannah and Veronica have joined us for the Thanksgiving weekend.

Pre-Thanksgiving Mom orders pizza for dinner. We sit at the dining room table, indulged in conversation that's centered around Ryan and me.

When did you guys reconnect? How did it happen? When did you decide to start dating again?

"How long did it take you all to start grinding?" Veronica snickers around chewing.

I turn and give her a fixed glare. Ryan squeezes my thigh. Everyone turns to us.

"So serious, you two! I'm just joking!" She waves us off.

"I tell you, that mouth of yours is going to get you in trouble, Veronica," Aunt Grace chastises.

"How are you liking North Carolina, Rose?" Ryan asks directing the conversation back into friendly territory.

I settle into my seat, watching the laughter, snide remarks, jeers, and high-fives. This bonding moment, prepping dishes, baking pies, playing dominoes till the wee hours of the night brings me joy. How seamlessly Ryan fits in.

I yawn, and head slumps onto Ryan's shoulder. I've been awake for over twelve hours; my mind lugs me into unconsciousness.

I awake as a moan escapes through my lips; my body squirms. I gasp at the sight of a dark head of hair bobbing between my legs. He sucks on my clit, twirls it with his tongue. He gently sucks on my folds. My hand anchors in his hair.

His fingers plunge inside me.

My breathing becomes labored. I can never get enough of his skillful tongue. The way his tongue

142

moves and explores. The amount of pleasure he can elicit with that one tool.

It's fucking amazing.

I grunt.

"Shhh …" His fingers stroke deeper. My channel becomes slicker.

The tip of his tongue invades me, slowly writing his name.

"Fuck," I whisper yell.

My legs quake, my body on the verge of explosion. Ryan abruptly stops.

"What are you doing!?" I stutter.

He cracks a smile. His shark-like moss eyes fill with need. He sits back on his knees, stroking his shaft. "Angel, I need you to be quiet while I fuck you. Can you do that?" His cock caresses my entrance.

"I will … try."

"You have to, babe. I am going to take you, and it isn't going to be gentle." He tortures me with his cock, rubbing, coating his cock with my essence. "I don't want to die. Sam is going to kill me if he catches me in here."

I bite my lip. My eyes dilate, wild with longing.

"I will try."

"Open your legs wider," he commands.

I do it without qualm. I yelp at his invasion. He places my legs on his shoulders. Going deeper, harder, faster.

I cry out.

He smothers my cries with his lips. He hits the g-spot over and over and over.

"Cum with me." He bites my ear.

I nod. His thumb rubs my core, arousing me more.

143

How is this even possible?

"Ryan!" I sob.

His head falls back; his mouth hangs open as he joins me over the cliff.

He pulls out of me and lays his head between my bosoms.

My eyes seal. I can feel his heartbeat, the abnormal drum, an immense pressure.

We stiffen at the thump in the hallway.

"I love you," I say. This may be the last time I am able to utter these words if Sam catches Ryan in my room, both of us butt naked.

Nah … he wouldn't open my room door, but he may open Ryan's.

Ryan nuzzles my neck and breasts as the sound lessens. "I can't believe I risked my life because I can't keep my hands off you for long."

I cackle, pushing Ryan from my bed. He smirks, hastily getting dressed.

The increased noise coming from the hallway alerts us that everyone is up. He was aware of the risk he took by coming to my room. Now the possibility of him getting caught doubles.

I feel the thrill and excitement I once did when Ryan and I snuck around Florida. That risk of getting caught.

What's the worst that can happen?

He kisses my lips and tiptoes to the door, humming the Mission Impossible theme song. He opens the door, surveys the hallway, then bolts.

I fall backward on the bed, bent in two.

Chapter Twenty-Seven

Ryan has awoken a dormant part of me. The woman that enjoys to live a little on the edge a little. The thrills I get from not playing it safe all the time. What I did with Ryan this morning, I wouldn't have done with anyone else. The risk is always too great unless I am risking it for him.

I am his, and he is mine. I love this man with everything within me. I love how he controls my body, how it goes haywire only for him. I see forever each time I gaze upon him. I see the love in him that I read about in romance books. The love that outlives one's lifetime.

I find Mom, Aunt Grace, Savannah, and Veronica hard at work in the kitchen. I walk outside in search of Ryan. I lean against the sliding door, ogling Ryan in the form fitting, corded, beige sweater.

How did I get so lucky?

The men sit outside with mugs of coffee, discussing the upcoming football games.

"Hey, little girl," Uncle Sam calls out. "Aren't you supposed to be in the kitchen with all the other women preparing our feast?" he says with a smart-ass smirk.

"Little." I glance over my shoulder, turning in a circle. "I don't see any little girl here, old, senile man. Did you forget your glasses or take your pills today? Memory loss is a bad and debilitating part of old age."

They crack up.

I love moments like this. Memories.

"Ryan, you need to speak to your girl. She should know that her place is in the kitchen. I hope you are not there spoiling her?" Uncle Frank bellows.

I bet Uncle Frank wouldn't say that shit in front of his wife.

I fold my arms, waiting for Ryan's response. Waiting to see if he would take the bait or be smart and shut up.

"Wench, aren't you going to go and prepare my feast? Get to it. I am famished, and so are my fellow good men."

My body shakes. I curtsey and bow my head. "I'll get right to it, me lord."

I walk back into the kitchen.

"That's what I am talking about. Next time, we let Ryan deal with it." Uncle Frank comments.

The dining room table is lined with an array of dishes; mac and cheese, sweet potatoes, ham, cranberry sauce, mofongo (green plantain turkey stuffing), Arroz con Gandules (Puerto Rican rice with pigeon peas). A blend of dishes from both my mom's heritage— Hispanic and black.

What's Dad having for Thanksgiving?

I plate a small amount of food, saving space to satisfy my sweet tooth.

I bounce to the kitchen counter, squeezing my palms together with glee.

It's such a hard choice. Do I want the pumpkin pie, apple pie, brownie, peach cobbler, coconut flan, Besitos de Coco (coconut kisses)?

I take a thick slice of each dessert. Balancing two plates of yumminess, I return back to the dining room. I moan, as the flavors of the peach cobbler dance on my tongue.

146

"I thought I'm the only one that can elicit that sound from you," Ryan whispers.

I shake my head no, pointing to the desserts.

A plate loaded with dessert can be unhealthy, but my body was built for this edacious event. I can always burn off the calories using The Mulligan.

"Wow! Simone, are you going to save any of the desert for us?" Savannah's voice echoes.

"Probably."

I smack Ryan's fork away from my plate.

"I don't understand how you can eat so muchsweets and not get fat." Veronica wrinkles her nose.

"There are many ways to work it off." I bite into a Besitos de Coco.

"Please, enlighten us on how you are able to accomplish this," she challenges with a lopsided grin.

"Well, Veronica … let's think." I tap my chin. "There are various methods you could find beneficial, such as …. walking, dancing and my absolute fave—riding."

Mom's fork suspends inches from her mouth, giving me a curious look. Ryan's eyes bulge, and he lowers his head, focused on his meal.

Mom still believes I am a virgin. She never found out I had sex with Ryan the night of sophomore prom; she still thinks I spent the night at Tinea's.

"Riding!?" Savannah asks, a devious gleam in her eye. "That sounds like an activity I would enjoy. Tell me … what type of riding do you enjoy—horse, exercise bike, or human?"

Unbelievable bitch. Talk about lack of decorum.

We are a traditional Catholic family. We don't talk like this. Veronica is trying to make me seem less than a proper lady in front of my mother.

I sneer at Veronica, baring my teeth.

Ryan chokes on his sip of wine. I slap his back.

"You okay?" I ask him. He turns pale.

His eyes water.

Savannah and Veronica hoot, tears streaming down their faces. Uncle Sam's nostrils flare, he stares at Ryan. The fire in his eyes speaks volumes.

Mom clears her throat.

"Exercise bike," I answer, with a cheesy grin.

Uncle Sam's and Mom's chests deflate at the same time. Color returns to Ryan's cheeks.

Before we know it, it's time to return to reality. Late nights studying, school, work, and falling asleep in Ryan's arms.

"It was nice having you here, Ryan." Mom hugs him and places a kiss on the side of his face.

"I'll see you in a couple weeks for Christmas." She pinches my cheeks.

I shuffle my feet.

"I'm … actually spending Christmas with Ryan in Florida."

Her face turns ghostly white.

Chapter Twenty-Eight

As Christmas Day approaches, tension builds in my limbs. My breathing becomes shallow and quick. Mrs. Mulligan is not a fan of mine. She never accepted the relationship between her son and me. Madeline, the daughter of her best friend, is the only girl she finds suitable for him.

Memories of the day she caught Ryan and me in the library accelerate in my mind; the coldness in her cornflower blue stare.

His family is expecting him to bring a friend home, but they are not expecting me. I pleaded with him to let them know, but he was persistent that it was better this way.

I jolt out of my sleep, nightmare—Ryan's mom kicking me out of her home after I caught Ryan and Madeline in throes of passion.

I gasp, my heart hammers. I curl up within myself on the bed. Ryan strokes my back. He kisses across my neck.

"Babe, calm down. It's not going to be bad. Nothing bad will happen."

"I can smell it; there is a chilly, tingle running through my spine."

"You're working yourself up for nothing. I know the thing to put you at ease." He rubs his cock against my butt.

He runs his hand up between my thighs, erasing all

thoughts and tension.

His cock cures all my ailments—headaches, backaches, stress, sleep deprivation. He touches me, and relief descends.

Our flight leaves La Guardia at 5:15 p.m. and arrives at PBI at 8:17 p.m. La Guardia is overcrowded, people traveling from near and far in a hurry to get to their destination. The agent announces that our flight is packed and commences boarding.

Note to self, never travel on Christmas Eve.

I settle into my seat, belt latched. The plane pushes back from the gate; the engine roars as it crawls down the runway, then it accelerates and the plane lifts off.

A mountain of cars is parked at the Mulligans' home. I turn to Ryan with wide eyes, gripped with fear.

Shit!

A memory materializes. My mother was in charge of many parties, especially during the holidays. Mom made the deserts while the other four courses were catered.

I sigh.

Great, just great.

The Christmas Eve party is a black and white affair. I am dressed in blue skinny jeans, a black sweater, and black ballet flats.

"Did you know about this!?"

"No, Angel. Mom didn't mention this."

I point to my attire.

"You look beautiful, don't stress about it." He

150

palms and kisses my hand. "Relax, I am in jeans and a t-shirt."

"That's easy for you to say. It's your parents, and they love you." He takes my hand as I exit the car. Ryan retrieves our bags from the trunk. Chatter and laughter greet us upon entering the Mulligans' home. Ryan walks us toward the noise. I pull my sweaty hands away, frozen behind a pillar.

"Surprise!" Ryan announces.

"Ryan!" his mom screeches.

"Welcome home, son."

I love him, but I can't do this.

My heart hammers in my chest. I feel as if I am going to black out. I bend over, head between my knees. I close my eyes and count to ten.

"Where is your friend?" Mrs. Mulligan asks.

Oh shit! Oh shit! I can't do this.

I stand, straighten my shoulders, and push air through my lips.

You love this man … be strong.

"My friend had a change of plans, but I found this beauty. I decided to bring her home instead."

He backs out of the dining room to find me hiding behind the pillar.

He shakes his head and tugs me to him.

I plant my feet. He jerks me harder.

"Hi." I wave, standing in view of the Mulligans and their guests.

"Oh my gosh! Is that Simone?" Mr. Mulligan asks. He stands from his chair and comes to greet me. He hugs me tightly and gives me a peck on the cheek. "It's so good to see you. All grown up and gorgeous."

"Thank you," I reply, heat rising in my cheeks.

I peek at Ryan's mother. A shiver runs through me

151

as our eyes meet.

"Well, let's get two extra seats," Mrs. Mulligan states to one of the caterers.

I do not recognize Madeline until I'm seated across from her.

Unf-ucking-believable. This night is getting better and better. My shoulders deflate.

"So good to see you, Simone." Venom streams from Madeline's words.

"Nice to see you, Madeline," I reply sweetly.

We arrive after appetizers are served. I will have to sit here and suffer through another four courses. I don't engage in the conversation around us.

The deserts do not compare to the ones I had for Thanksgiving; the pieces are small and the options limited.

The tiramisu, strawberry cheesecake, and Chocolate brownies sit on my plate.

"My goodness, Ryan. I'm so happy you found Simone and brought her for dinner. Poor thing is hungry," Madeline chides.

I tilt my head; we look fixedly at each other.

The words sit on the tip of my tongue, but my brain overrules my heart, reminding me of my surroundings.

I look over at Ryan; I shudder at the way he glares at her.

"Do not hide your sarcasm with disrespect, Madeline. I won't let you speak to my girlfriend that way," he snaps at her.

I squeeze his thigh, and he looks down at me.

My eyes crinkle.

"Ryan, I was just joking," she fakes innocence. "Touchy, touchy, aren't we? Sooooo protective of your Simone."

"Madeline," he snaps.

"Come on, you two, get it together," Ryan's mother's sturdy voice echoes.

"I love you, sorry about her," Ryan mouths.

I bat my lashes.

The Christmas Eve party starts to dissipate at 11:00 p.m. Ryan speaks with the guests before taking my hand and retreating to his room.

"Your parents are okay with me staying in your room?"

"I don't care."

"You don't?"

"Babe, I am a grown man. I am visiting my parents; I don't live here."

I take a shower in his suite, washing off the day, praying that Christmas Day will be better.

Ryan stands in the doorway as I walk out of the shower.

"Sim, I'm going to have a couple drinks with my old man."

"Okay, I'm going to sleep." I yawn.

He walks over and brushes his lips against mine.

"I will find a fun way to wake you up when I get back."

"You are so nasty." I giggle.

I pound the pillow, tossing and turning in the bed. My body is drained, but my brain refuses to shut off. Maybe it's the uneasiness of being in this house without Ryan.

A glass of warm milk will help you to sleep.

I tiptoe down the stairs, not wanting to disturb Mrs. Mulligans.

I pour a glass of milk and warm it in the microwave.

"Ahhh, I see that you could not sleep either."

Chapter Twenty-Nine

"Aaahhh." I jump at the sound of Mrs. Mulligan's voice. I turn to find her standing in the entrance of the kitchen.

Oh gosh! What is she doing here? I know it's her house, but shit.

I am weary of her presence and being alone with her. Memories of Mrs. Mulligan catching Ryan and me come to the surface of my mind. It cuts through the happiness and invades my confidence in our relationship.

During dinner, it seemed that her attention was directed to Madeline's mom; but I knew her ears were sitting in the middle of the conversation between Ryan and Madeline. Her face was screwed up as if she had bitten a sour lime.

I shouldn't care about her opinion of me; Ryan says that all the time. Ryan values his parents' opinions although he pretends not to at times. He has done everything his parents have asked of him. He excels in school, sports, and learning the ropes of the family business from the ground up. Someday he will be expected to run the second largest architectural firm in the country.

"Sorry, did I wake you? I couldn't sleep so I came down to grab a glass of milk." I hold the glass up.

"What are you doing with my son?" Daggers flow

from her eyes.

Why does she despise me so much?

Typically, I like to get to the point and not beat around the bush. In this situation, I wish she would have made small talk, warmed me up a little, and made me feel a smidge comfortable. That's not her though. I respect that.

"We are dating."

"When did this all start?" Her eyebrows draw together.

"October."

"How did he find you?"

What? I frown. "What do you mean, how did he find me?"

"Don't be crass with me, Simone. How did you guys find each other?" I pull back as if she physically slapped me.

"Tinea ran into him, and she invited him to her birthday party."

I am being cross examined, questions rapidly coming at me.

"The deal was for you to stay away from him. Is the money not enough?" she yells, veins protruding in her neck.

My heart gallops. My limbs tremble. The words out of her mouth make no sense.

"You lost me. What money are you talking about?"

"Don't act stupid. You know about the money I gave your mom."

I shake my head.

"You gave my mom money? For what purpose? What the hell are you talking about?" I scream.

A sheen of sweat covers my back. Adrenaline crashes through me. My heart palpitates so hard it feels like it might explode. My eyes widen. I grab onto the kitchen counter to prevent me from falling.

This isn't real. I went to sleep, and I need to wake up.

I want to run but instead I remain. I need to learn about the money, my mom's role in all this, and how this correlates to my relationship with Ryan.

"Stop acting stupid, Simone." She walks toward me. "The money I gave your mother to keep you away from my son." Her finger elongates. "He is not going to marry the likes of you. I could see my friends laughing now. Oh look, Ryan married the maid's daughter. Over my dead body. He will be with someone in his league. Someone that will help him when he becomes CEO," she sneers.

The harsh scent of alcohol oozes out of her mouth.

"Are you back for more money? I gave her enough! I mean, three quarters of a million. That should have been enough to get you nicely settled and far away from my son."

Wow!

I back away from her, needing to reclaim my personal space. I am being suffocated by her crippling words. I take heavy breaths to allow my body to partially function.

Mom told me we were moving due to Uncle Sam's new job. *Was that all a lie? She uprooted me my senior year because this witch paid her off.* We moved within weeks. Six months after moving, Mom opened a bakery. A year later, she bought the house.

Was all of this purchased with blackmail money? How could she have taken it?

I knew Mrs. Mulligans didn't like me, but I wouldn't think she would go this far.

I have to get out of here.

I throw the cold milk away and storm out of the kitchen. I snatch my bag out of Ryan's closet.

"Hey, babe."

I still at the sound of Ryan's voice.

"Simone, what the hell are you doing?" He grabs my hand.

"Why are you packing?"

A cry forces itself out of me. Beads of salt run into my mouth. I swipe my hand across my cheeks.

"I can't stay here. I have to leave," I plead. "Please, Ryan, I can't stay in this house."

He hooks his finger under my chin, bringing our eyes face to face.

"What happened?"

"Ask your mom."

His jaw clenches. He kisses my pale skin. I see the storm brewing in his cloudy, green eyes. He charges out of his room.

I can hear their raised voices from the top of the stairs.

"What the hell is going on here?" Mr. Mulligan yells.

"Tell your wife to stay the hell out of my life," Ryan roars.

"Ryan, she is not right for you." Mrs. Mulligan yells.

I walk down the steps with my bag in hand.

"That's the woman I love, and you don't get to make that decision."

I pause in the hallway after hearing him say those words.

"But, Ryan …" Mrs. Mulligan screeches.

"Stay out of my life." He comes around the corner like a bulldozer.

"Babe, stay right here. Let me get my stuff."

My shoulders sigh with relief.

"Christina, what did you do?" Mr. Mulligan asks his wife.

"I did what I had to do, Joe. That girl isn't good enough for our son," she huffs.

"I told you to leave that boy alone. Let him make his own decisions. Something I wish I was allowed to do."

"Joe …"

Chapter Thirty

Hot lava boils deep in my system. My mind is baffled. The abandonment I feel by my mother. Her betrayal. She pulled the wool over my eyes. She told me to stand my ground, don't let anyone push me around. Be proud of who I am and where I come from. Be a proud Hispanic, black, and white woman.

You can't tell my ethnicity at first glance. My olive skin tone, long brunette hair, and almond shaped hazel eyes. Many see me as a white woman, until they meet my mom.

Be proud of who you are, Simone. Never let anyone make you feel lesser than.

Anger, confusion, humiliation, betrayal, and shame intertwines. I lay my head on the breakfast table, reflecting on the origins of these feelings.

"Hey, girl. What's going on with you?" Tinea rubs my arm.

I shrug.

"You have been isolating yourself lately. Your energy is off."

I shrug.

"You lost your voice."

I shrug.

"Is there something going on with you and Ryan?"

I sigh.

She pulls out the chair and sits next me.

"Hey, you are worrying me." She rubs my back in a

circular motion. "Do you need me to call your mom or Ryan?"

I shake my head no.

"Whenever you are ready to talk, I'm here." She weakly smiles. She kisses my hair and goes to get ready for her day.

I have been living in a bubble of depression. Christmas Eve was officially the second worst day of my life. Learning about the money that my mom took from Ryan's mom has left me in a haze.

Ryan and I left his parent's home on Christmas morning. We spent Christmas Day at the Breakers Hotel and flew back to New York the following day.

We hadn't planned on being back in New York until after the New Year. Tinea was splitting her holiday time, half with her family and the latter half with Craig's. Jackie went to the islands.

The apartment is desolate and quiet. I used to enjoy quiet moments; the exciting ideas that spin in my mind. Daydreaming about the life Ryan and I would build.

The days of escaping into the pages of a new romance novel have disappeared; now the quiet only brings me torment. My mind has pressed repeat on the events of Christmas Eve—there's no pause or stop button in sight.

I gathered a few clothing and toiletries my second day back, figuring Ryan can occupy my mind in a pleasurable way, shutting off the voices.

That plan failed. Ryan decided to return to work, leaving me in his apartment during the day with my thoughts.

Work.

I picked up a couple shifts at the café, and I volunteered to fill in whenever needed.

This placed a wrench in Ryan's plans for us to go to the Hamptons New Year's Eve night.

I keep taking extra shifts after school begins. The more I am occupied, the thoughts of that day stayed in the shadows.

I make the choice not to speak with my mother or divulge the information I had learned to Ryan. Three weeks, and I'm still trying to come to terms with it all.

The café gets busy in droves. The weekend provides relief from the non-stop lines we get during the week.

The soles of my feet ache when 4 p.m. rolls around. I have been on my feet since noon. I buy a small mocha and sit in the corner, giving my aching feet some relief.

My phone chimes.

Ri: What time do you get off?
Sim: 6
Ri: Okay

I stare at my phone, waiting for additional communication, but nothing comes.

My mind begins to twist and turn, suffocating me with questions.

Did Mom agree with Mrs. Mulligan that I'm not good enough for Ryan? Does she think that I am less than them? Why would she take the money? I would have told the bitch to fuck off. Mom's facial expression when I told her that I was spending Christmas in Florida makes perfect sense now. Even then, she had the time to call and tell me not to go. She could have prevented the humiliation that I endured. I don't know how I can forgive her for this. She's the only one I have, and she did this to me.

I ward off the falling tears.

"Simone, help Jerod with inventory, please," says my coworker, Julie.

I tally the number of bags of roasted coffee beans the cafe still has on hand.

161

"Simone, Mr. Fine Ass is here." Julie smiles and her eyes widen.

"Thanks. Let him know I'll be there in a minute."

Five minutes later, Jerod and I have the inventory completed. I hand him the figures I had jotted down.

"Hey, babe." I walk up to Ryan and kiss his lips.

"Hey. You ready to go?"

"Yeah, let me take off the apron and grab my bag."

I sling the bag across my shoulder. "See you guys Monday." I wave goodbye to my coworkers.

"I'm surprised to see you."

"I haven't seen you all week, babe. I miss you." He kisses the side of my head and wraps his hand on my shoulder and brings me flush against him. "I'm taking you out to dinner."

"Aaaa … can we just not go to dinner tonight? I'm exhausted."

"Yeah, babe, we can go to my house and order dinner."

"Can we go to my place instead?"

He lets out a harsh breath. "Let's do my place tonight."

I nod.

It's a quick, quiet ride back to Ryan's.

"I'm going to take a quick shower. Order me shrimp teriyaki and miso soup," I say shortly after entering the penthouse.

We sit at the kitchen island eating our meal. There is an eerie silence that hangs above us. I glance at him

162

from the corner of my eye.

"You are normally so talkative. Are you okay?" he asks me.

"Yeah, just tired."

He huffs, places his fork down on the counter, and turns my chair toward him.

"We just need to talk about this and get it over with."

I furrow my eyebrows. "Get what over with?"

"What you and my mother spoke about."

"We didn't speak. She spoke."

"What did she say?"

Do I really want to talk about this? I don't. I just want to hide from it.

"I don't want to discuss it."

He breathes loud as he rubs his hands over his face. "You have been slowly pulling away from me. When we came back, I thought we were good, but we're not. I know you, Simone. Little by little, you are pulling away." He takes my hands in his, rubbing his thumb along my knuckles. "We haven't seen each other in a week. If I didn't show up at your job today, we wouldn't be together now."

"I have been busy with school, work, and study group." I pull my hands away.

"What did she say?"

I know that he will not let this go. I cave and answer his question.

"Your mother …" I watch as his emotions elevate from worry, to confusion, the wind around him growing fast and fierce into full steam rage.

"She fucking did what!?" He hops off the chair. He paces back and forth through the kitchen.

"What the hell did Rose say when you confronted

163

her about this?"

I bite my nail. "I haven't spoken to her about it yet."

"Why the hell not? Our moms are fucking with our lives."

"I know that," I whisper. I look around the kitchen. He turns my face to his.

"Why haven't you said anything? You haven't spoken to Rose since then?"

I nod my head yes. "I texted her New Year's Day. That's it. I have been ignoring her calls."

"We need to talk with her; there is more to this than what my mother said."

He touches his head to mine. "I think I have been avoiding her. If I talk with her, this all becomes real," I admit.

"It's already real, babe. You've been suffering with that information and I've been paying for it. This is why you have been distancing yourself from me." He kisses my forehead.

I pull myself away from him. I stand and walk to the couch. "I have been thinking a lot." I fiddle with my necklace. "I have been thinking that maybe we are not supposed to be."

"What the fuck did you just say?" He storms over to me. I feel his breath on my face. "You're shitting me with this bullshit. You did hear me tell her that I fucking love you, right?" he roars.

I jump. "I'm going …" I point toward the front door.

He slams his lips to mine, kissing me furiously. He sucks on my bottom lip. His hands caress my stomach. His lips swallows mine, he pushes his tongue into my mouth.

My nipples harden. His hand slowly moves up my

stomach. My back collapses on the couch. I moan into his mouth.

He climbs on top of me.

Relax, Simone. Clear your mind. This may be the last time you get to enjoy every inch of him.

I hold him tightly against me. I take my time running my hands all over his back. I lower my hands and squeeze his firm ass.

He lifts my sweatshirt over my head; wraps his mouth around one nipple, while playing with the other.

I grind my hips into his.

My mind clears, reveling in euphoria.

Chapter Thirty-One

Your first love, or lust, your imagination
   falling for the thoughts of your infatuation.
   Pushing for the things your mind wants to be
   acting on the thoughts of your mentality.

It's all good for a second, be real
   if you can pass that stage, you can start to feel.
   Battling the wars as you begin to see
   learning that lust isn't what love is meant to be.

If it was easy it wouldn't take so much time
   it's a battle both physically and in the mind.
   The hardships and struggles ma and pa didn't tell
you about
   the difference between years and months is simply
your mouth.

Is this destiny or destined to be?
    can your imagination come together with your
reality?
    After time, it shows the best and worst part of you
    this can only last, if you really want it to.

                                    Just Jon

Chapter Thirty-Two

Five years later

Tinea and I sit in the fourth row behind the Jayhawks bench, our eyes barely on the basketball game. Instead, our minds are occupied with Tinea's upcoming nuptials.

"Dad is driving me nuts. He wants to add another ten people to the guest list," Tinea pouts. "I don't know three quarters of these people. Is it my wedding or a celebration for my dad?"

"Girl, stop stressing. It will be okay. He's picking up the check." I whistle. "Over a million."

"So! That doesn't mean he can invite anyone he wants to. Between family and friends for both Craig and me, we were at seventy-five people. The guest list is up to two-fifty." She sighs.

I blink. My eyes widen. "Two-hundred and fifty? Maybe have Craig talk with him?"

She giggles. "Craig is putty in Dad's hands. He's going to come back to me and say 'Babe, two-sixty isn't that bad.' We should have eloped."

I give her a weird look. "First, you wouldn't be happy with that. Two, your mom would murder you."

"Yeah, I know."

"It's in two weeks. It will be fine. This is about you and Craig, at the end of the day. Everything will be perfect."

"I know," she squeals. "I'm getting married."

I laugh. I am happy for her. She knew that Craig was the one for her and went all in. He loves her unconditionally. He spoils her, but he's not afraid to check her at the same time. She needs that or she would walk all over him.

"How do you feel about seeing Ryan? It's been almost five years."

"It will be good seeing him. I'll be fine. He's moved on with his life, and I am with that fine ball player." I point to Samuel Dixon, the center for the New York Jayhawks. My sexy boyfriend.

She shakes her head. "Keep saying that to yourself; maybe it will be true by my wedding."

Yeah, the witch is right. I am anxious.

The wedding is in Florida. I'm Tinea's maid of honor, and Ryan is Craig's best man. It will be the first time that we have seen each other since we spilt for a second time.

The feeling of abandonment. The shadows that lingered in the bottom of my mind. The unforgiving pain. The heartbreak. The ghost of the emotions I felt when Ryan and I first broke up didn't linger this time. Enthralled in school and work, the ghost became nothing. Leaving me slightly stronger from the weeks before and ready to move on.

I recall how I slowly continued to close off pieces of me from Ryan after telling him about what our moms did. We tried to make our relationship work— actually, he tried as I became more withdrawn.

We went from spending nights together, sex several times a week, texting each other invariably, to nothing.

I sit on my bed, legs crossed, typing away on my laptop. A knock sounds at the door.

"You can come in."

Ryan walks in. His eyes are dull and lack sparkle. His expression hardens. He stands, his arms folded, feet apart.

His eyes narrow. "I had to see with my own eyes that you were fine."

I give him a confused look. "What do you mean by that?"

"We haven't spoken in three days."

"Oh. I have been so busy with school. The days just flowed into each other. Sorry about that. How are you?"

"Are you fucking real?" He cocks his head to the side. "That's a stupid ass question, Simone."

I search for the right words to say to him. I see the hurt that I have unintentionally caused. The sadness I have put into the man that I love.

I lift my head up to the ceiling. Tears stream down my face.

"What do you want, Simone?"

"I don't know." That's my honest answer. I still haven't confronted my mom and asked her about the money. That money is a dark cloud hanging over my head, and shattering my heart.

"You don't know? Your actions are telling me that you don't want us. You are letting what our moms did fucking destroy us." His voice escalates.

"Tell me what to do. What do you want?" I shyly

look at him.

"Talk with your mother, and deal with it. Let our love continue to grow. We move on with our lives. It's not going to be easy. I know you, you run when our relationship gets hard. You are afraid. You let the negative thoughts and darkness take over." He walks to the edge of the bed, leans into my personal space. "Let me be your light switch—your energy, your vision, the one to ignite rich colors back into you when the darkness comes." He pushes my hair back from my face.

I'm so not worthy of this man.

"Every time I look at myself in the mirror or I look at you, the thoughts that run through me ... it's not pleasing. The fact that your mom most likely paid for my tuition with the contingency of me staying out of your life. She paid for the house we live in, she's paid for our life in North Carolina. What else will she do?"

"Who gives a fuck?"

"I do." I look away from his glare. "I do."

"Again, I ask. What ... do ... you ... want?"

What do you want, Simone?

"To go on our separate paths. Come summer, you will be moving to Boston to start Harvard. I will be busy with my internship at Rhodes Agency and finishing up my final year. We are on different paths."

"Really." His voice drops an octave. "You can so easily throw us away."

"No, this isn't easy for me." I cup his face. "I am putting gashes in my heart, but it's the best thing for both of us now."

"You're so damn stubborn. I can't even get you to change your mind. FUCK." He stands back.

I close my eyes at his angry glare.

171

I hear the door open and slammed.

I leave him again out of fear. Yet he loved me despite all my faults. He loved me for me. I will love him till infinity.

Later that night, I pick up my cell phone and called my mom. I haven't spoken to her since I texted her on New Year's Day. There are multiple missed calls and unanswered text messages from my mom and Uncle Sam. I refused to acknowledge them.

My mom has struggled as a single mother. She was ecstatic when she got the job with the Mulligans, she didn't need to work two jobs anymore. She would have some time to spend with me at night. I have asked myself what I would have done if I was in her position. Would I have taken the money?

No.

In all fairness, it's easier for me to think that since I am not the one in the position.

"Mija," Mom answers, choked up.

"Hi," I whisper.

"Are you okay?" she asks.

"Should I be?" I run my hand through my hair.

She doesn't answer.

"The look on your face when I told you I was spending Christmas with the Mulligans—I got an inkling that you knew something or didn't approve of me going there. Yet, you said nothing to me. I was walking into the lion's den, and you didn't stop me, Mom."

"I didn't know how to tell you."

"It's easy to tell me that you lied. Uncle Sam's job wasn't the reason why we left. You could have been honest with me. She gave you money, and you took it."

"What was I supposed to do? Mija, she fired me.

172

She told me that she could fire me and I could continue living in the state or I could take the money and leave willingly. I had you to think about." She let out a heavy breath. "I took it and the chance for us to start over. I could put away money and pay for your college. You wouldn't have to worry about student loans. I did what I had to do. I did what was best for us." She sighs into the phone.

"You didn't think I was good enough for Ryan?"

"Simone, I would never think that. You are gorgeous inside and out. Any man will be fortunate to have you in their life."

"I lost the man I love over this."

"Mija, if it is meant to be in the future, it will be. Nothing or no one will be able to stop the two of you."

Yeah, only myself and my fears.

"I'm still going to need some time to deal with what you did. I hear you and understand that you did what you thought was right. You still should have told me and prepared for me that shit show. I will forgive you and move forward. You are the only mother I have," I assure her.

I spent that summer getting coffee, lunch, photocopying, and pitching ideas for campaigns for which I got no credit. Still, I woke excited each morning to work at the Rhodes Agency. At the end of the year, Rhodes would extend job offers to two interns and I was vying to be one of the two chosen.

Since then, I have worked as a junior account

173

executive, senior account executive, and now at my current position: creative director.

My team worked on a new sneaker campaign for Soles. I met Samuel Dixon, the 6'3', chocolate god at the launch party. We immediately hit it off and have been together for two years.

Sam will be accompanying me to Tinea's wedding. He has a game the day of the rehearsal dinner. He will be flying in for the wedding that Saturday.

Until then, I have to face the love of my life alone.

Chapter Thirty-Three

"What?" I yell. "Tinea?"

I stomp toward her at the front of the makeshift altar.

"What the hell? Why am I walking down the aisle with Ryan?" I shriek.

She shrugs. "That's what we want." She points to her fiancé, Craig.

I point back and forth between us. "I see you."

"Me." She puts her hand up.

Craig walks over; his arm circles his soon-to-be wife. "What's up, Simone?"

"You know what's up." I glare at him. "I am walking down the aisle with Ryan." I fold my arms.

"It's what the wife wants." He kisses her neck.

I growl.

"It's her wedding, Simone, be nice." He smirks.

"Oh, I'm so nice. But I see you, witch. So damn lucky I love your ass." I walk away.

"Okay, ladies and gentleman, lets run through this," the wedding coordinator announces.

You can get through this.

I say these words over and over until they coat my entire body. I walk to the back of the park and stand in the line.

After all, this weekend isn't about me. It's a celebration of Tinea and Craig's love for each other. We all came to Florida to celebrate and share in this new journey with my best friend.

I watch as the other bridesmaids and groomsmen stroll up the aisle. Ryan and I, maid of honor and best man, are the last ones to go. We stand next to each other.

"Hi," Ryan says.

"Hello."

"We don't have to make this awkward. We can speak to each other."

"I know."

"How've you been?" he asks as we saunter down the aisle.

"Good." The desire to end the conversation is written on my face.

We separate to our respective spots on the makeshift altar. I exhale. I didn't realize I was holding my breath.

"That was great! Let's run through it once more, and then we can call it a wrap." The coordinator claps her hands.

Just great.

The exchange between Ryan and I comes to mind as I get dressed for the rehearsal dinner. He is still the sexiest man I have ever seen. His dark brown hair is brushed from his face. His chiseled jaw, and glowing, emerald eyes. The sound of his husky, velvet voice. He's dressed in black jeans and a white dress shirt with his sleeves rolled up to his elbows. His muscles ripple beneath his clothes as he walks. He is still charming and sexy as hell. Everything about him is sharp.

I could have sworn I saw a hint of a tattoo on his forearm. My panties dampen.

I exam myself in the mirror.

I look damn good. Sam would love this outfit.

I fluff the big curls in my hair. The blush dress with its cowl neckline, fitted bodice, and high slit on the right wraps and emphasizes my body in the right ways.

I enter the ballroom where the rehearsal dinner is being held and zero in on Ryan.

I stand at the entrance, speechless at the sight of Madeline seated next to him.

He's with her.

It takes me a minute to pick my face up off the ground. I watch him from the corner of my eye as I walked to my seat. The room is filled with the seventy-five people Tinea had intended to invite before it ballooned to two hundred and sixty-three

Two long tables seating forty people each are occupied with the bride and groom's families and close friends. The middle of the tables are covered with a beige runner. Varying sizes of floral arrangements and candles sit intermediately in a row on each table.

The arrangements are sublime.

"God damn, Simone. Come sit over here by Uncle Bob," Craig's touchy-feely uncle calls.

I look at Uncle Bob over my shoulder. I shake my finger.

"Girl, you are so fine."

I walk over to him.

"Ain't she beautiful? She's going be my fourthwife."

I laugh. "Yeah, okay." I give him a kiss on his bald head. "You funny. Hi, Marie." I waive to this current wife. "Good seeing you too, Bob."

I turn and take a seat next to Tinea.

Ryan and Madeline sit a couple of seats away. My eyes keep traveling to them during the dinner. From the corner of my eye, I watch them. One corner of

Ryan's mouth curves up. He bends down, whispering in her ears.

His eyes catch mine watching. He continues to whisper in her ears as he stares at me. I am trapped by his lustful eyes. Although I want to look away, I can't bring myself to do it.

He bites her ear.

I swallow the lump stuck in my throat. I smile so hard my cheeks hurt as I stifle the well of tears desperate to spill.

Keep it together.

I pull away and smile at Tinea's cousin.

During dessert, Tinea and Craig walk around the room catching up with family and meeting with new ones.

Craig sits back, talking to his best man. I drag Tinea along with me to wish Craig farewell until tomorrow.

"Babe, we are leaving," she says and plants her ass in Craig's lap.

"Tinea, no strippers." Craigs scowls at me.

"What happens tonight is none of your business. It's the last time for us to get wild. Dicks can swing." I bend over in laughter at the look on Craig's face.

"Babe, let me go. She is just joking," Tinea protests.

Ryan shakes his head.

"Hi, Simone," Madeline chimes in.

"Hello." I give her a fake smile.

My eyes travel to the door. "Come on, the other ladies are waiting for us."

"See you tomorrow, Mrs. Clarke."

"I can't wait, Mr. Clarke." She kisses him.

I sit in semi silence as we drive to downtown Miami. My mind is whirling. How long have they been dating? Does he make love to her like he did to me? Does he plan to marry her? Is he with her to spite me?

"Hey, bitch, snap out of it. It's my bachelorette party," Tinea screams and hands me a shot of vodka.

The day has arrived. I awake a little hung over.

Thank God for these black-out curtains.

I sigh. I rest my hand on my head. The clock reads 10 a.m. I roll out of bed, shower, wash my hair, and get dressed in my pink sweatsuit. The word "maid of honor" is bedazzled on the back. I search my purse and find two pain killers. I swallow them then head downstairs for a light breakfast.

The bridal party leaves at 11:30 a.m. for a mani and pedi appointment. An hour and a half later, we ride the elevator to the suite where two makeup artists and two hairstylists await us.

Tinea is cheerful and happy. We talk and laugh about the events of the previous night.

I get a text from Samuel at 2:00 p.m. that he has arrived.

Before I know it, I'm dressed and helping Tinea put her wedding dress on.

The outside wedding ceremony is marvelous. The bridal party dances into the reception hall to screams and applause. Ryan pulls my chair out then takes his on the other side of where Craig will sit.

Everyone roars with cheers as the emcee announces the bride and groom.

Then, on to the beginning of toasts. Tinea and Craig's parents speak first. Ryan's speech elicits laughter and claps.

Your speech ain't going to compare.

The emcee calls me next. I stand, my legs a little shaky.

"Hi, I'm Simone. You can tell I'm the maid of honor based on my seating. Tinea and I met in middle school. She was the girl with spunk and flare. I was the quiet one. She walks up to me one day and says 'you're quiet; Mom says I'm always too loud, so we will be a good balance." I look around the room. "We have been two peas in a pod ever since then. She is always there for me, no matter the reason. Whenever I get intomy moods—and I do get them, this is only time I willclaim it— she knows to give me space. She doesn't abandon me but lurks in the corner waiting for me to come back out to play. I love you for that." I throw hera kiss. "She met this one," I point to Craig, "on her twenty-first birthday. That one brought him." I point to Ryan shaking my head. "Next thing I knew, she wastelling me she'd found her happily ever after. I have had a window to watch them water their relationship and to see it blossom and bloom. It is a beautiful thingto watch. Not to sound cheesy, but your love is something I aspire to have one day." I lift my wine glass. "To real fairytales and happily ever afters"

I hug Tinea and take my seat.

We watch the happy couple dance and laugh. Their love brightens the room. As other couples join the happy couple on the dance floor, I take the chance to go to the bathroom and gather my emotions.

I exit the ladies' room to find Ryan in his black Burberry tux leaning against the wall.

Oh gosh, this man exudes sex.

I briefly look at him and head back to the reception.

I can't comprehend the smirk on his face, and quite frankly, I don't care to find out.

"Simone, stop." He tugs on my hand. His touch is like a live electric wire. A feeling I don't feel with Sam.

"How can I help you?" I ask, wary of where this will lead.

"Give me a second?"

I hesitate to answer.

"Please stop," he begs.

He holds my hand as we walk in the opposite direction of the reception. We enter an office. Ryan locks the door.

He takes his jacket off and drops it to the ground. He picks me up. My legs instantly wrap around him. His hands are all over my body. His eyes are dilated. He turns, and my back hits the wall. His mouth obliterates mine. It is what I needed.

I moan. I place my hand into his pants, massaging his already thick cock.

I want him to fuck me so badly.

His hands are still caressing and probing my body. His lips kiss down the side of my face.

I arch my body toward him. His finger tucks up my dress.

"Stop playing with it and take my dick out."

I happily do it. I fumble with opening his pants. He pulls his hips back to give me better access.

He rips my thong, the material snaps against me. Without warning, he impales me with his large dick.

I cry out. It feels so right.

"You feel it. No one will ever make you feel this good." He bites my lips.

He fucks me hard and deep. His hands tightened on my ass cheeks. He pumps and pumps.

I moan.

A crescendo builds. I scream his name on the top of my lungs.

"Let them know who owns this pussy."

He roars, climaxing buried to hilt inside me.

He pulls out of me as he slowly lowers me to the ground, and tucks himself back into his pants. I straighten my dress.

My legs shake.

"What did we just do?"

"I fucked you." He laughs as he runs his thumb across my bottom lip.

"My boyfriend and your girlfriend are down the hall." I shove him.

"Madeline isn't my girlfriend; she's a friend."

"You guys are not together? Why did you bring her?" I wonder out loud. "Don't answer that. I don't really care."

"Why are you with that guy? You don't love him."

"I love him."

"Tell me you're in love with him." He backs me up into the wall. "Tell me."

"I love him," I whimper.

His jaw clenches. "You are not in love with him. Why are you wasting your time? Instead of being with the one you love."

"I love him," I repeat.

"You are a fucking coward." He points his finger in my face. "You run when things get difficult. You are in love with me, but you are scared that I'm going to leave you like your dad did."

"Fuck you, Ryan," I yell. "How dare you?"

"Why the hell do I keep coming after you, yearning for you? I deserve better. I deserve better than you."

He walks away.

His words cut me deep.

He's right.

"Shut the fuck up," I yell at my inner voice.

I return to the reception to find Ryan dancing with Madeline. I look around in search of Sam.

"Hey, babe, where have you been?"

"Talking with a friend outside."

Sam looks at me knowingly.

"Let's go dance."

I nod.

Sam and I slow dance to a few songs. Sucking in a breath, I stand still as he lowers to one knee. The music halts. The crowd turns towards us.

"You are the best thing that has ever happened to me. You are gentle, kind, caring, and forgiving. You are everything I look for in a woman. My journey wouldn't be complete without you. Simone, will you marry me?"

I scan all the faces, stopping at Ryan's.

He mouths. "Say no, say no."

I look back at Sam. "Yes."

Chapter Thirty-Four

The phone on my desk beeps.

"Yes," I answer.

"Simone, Tinea is on the line one for you." Rachel, my assistant, announces.

"Thanks, Rach." I switch and press one on the phone.

"Hi, Mrs. Clarke, how was the honeymoon?" I smile, taking a drink of my lukewarm coffee.

"Too short. Tahiti was magical. The food, the water, the sex ... the sex." Tinea sighs.

I laugh. "I bet it was good. Did you guys leave the room?"

"Girl, the last three days we went out."

"Watch, I'm going to hear you are pregnant in a month."

"Probably." She giggles. "We want to take our time though. Enjoy being newlyweds."

"Have you gone back to work yet?" I look over at the mood board on my desk. There is something missing. I need to get a meeting together with the team.

"No, no. I am going to start back next week. You available for lunch today?"

"Yeah, we can do something. Let's say two." I can have Rach schedule a meeting for four.

"Two works. Lily's Bistro's on 34th?"

"Italian sounds great. You know I'm always up for lasagna. See you in a bit." I hang up the phone. I look up at the clock; the time reads 11:30. I open my email, getting ready to notify the team about the last-minute meeting.

Alex barges into my office. "Do you have the mockup for the Peterson account available?"

I force a smile, sit back in my chair, fold my arms. "Do I report to you?"

"What?" She waves me off. "I have an idea that I think would work great. You should be appreciative for the help."

Why does she try me?

"I am appreciative of your constant need to help, but I got this." I give her a sweet smile. "Now, I got to get back to work."

Bitch.

I learned my lesson. Alexandra Goodman started at the agency a year after I did. She worked as a creative director. I got to know her once I was promoted to creative director. She came across as friendly, we had a few drinks and dinner after work. I found her a great resource to bounce ideas off of. That's until I ran an idea by her for a campaign that she miraculously presented in our staff meeting one week later.

I ceased all socialization with Alex from that point forward. I remain cordial and professional. I thought about confronting her, but what was the use? She is the CEO's granddaughter.

"Sorry I'm late." I give Tinea a sideways hug. Tinea is on her first glass of Moscato. I sit on the chair across

185

from her and picked up the menu. Although I know what I'm ordering, I still like perusing the menu to see if something else will catch my tastebuds.

Shortly after being seated, the hostess approaches the table. "Would you like to order a drink?" she asks.

"Yes, may I please have an iced tea?" I say, looking up from the menu. "Are you ready to order, T? I am starving." Tinea nods. "I will have lasagna." Tinea orders shrimp pasta and another glass of Moscato.

Tinea props her elbow on the table, a mischievous gleam in her eyes.

"How have you been, with that big rock on your finger?"

"Oh, this old thing. It's so heavy." My left hand goes lax. My nonexistent dimples try to appear.

"Did you see that coming?"

"It was out of left field. Yeah, we have been together for two years. I just didn't see it coming."

"I saw the look on your face. For people that don't know you, they thought you were ecstatic. I saw the fear in your eyes." She glares at me. "Why did you look at Ryan? Were you waiting for him to answer?"

My throat closes up.

"Ah … it was an automatic reaction." I divert my eyes to the booth across from us.

"What happened when you both disappeared?"

"What!?" I cough, choking on my glass of iced tea. I wipe my mouth with a napkin.

"Don't play games. What happened?" She crosses her arms.

I tense and sit back. If I knew this was going to be an inquisition, I wouldn't have come. I clear my throat.

"We had sex." I wipe the table of imaginary crumbs. "Some not so nice choice words were said."

"What did you say?"

We pause as the hostess places our meals on the table. The lasagna provides me with warm comfort that this conversation lacks.

"Why do you automatically think it's me!?" I snap.

"It's Ryan, and you are always trying to find the worst in your relationship so that you can run."

"Wow." I look up at the ceiling. "You sound just like him. He said that I run because I'm scared that he is going to leave me like my dad did." "Is he right?"

I shrug. My chest becomes heavy.

"I love you. You know that." She gives me a side smirk. "He's right, Simone." I flinch.

She pauses and looks deadpan into my hazel eyes. "I was shocked that you said yes to Samuel. When you glanced over at Ryan, I felt relief that you were going to do the right thing and tell Sam no. Then you said yes. Like hell, what the fuck? You don't love him. You are comfortable. You know if he broke up with you, you wouldn't be as devastated. You would be sad, yes, but you would brush it off and move forward. Hell, you wouldn't let it get that far. You always leave the guys first."

"Okay, you done?"

"No, I am not done. You need to seek out a therapist to deal with the mental emotions you battle with because of your dad. It's the only way you will be able to have a healthy relationship."

"Bitch, I have a healthy relationship." I point between us.

She snorts while smiling. "I am not fucking you, though."

"I hear what you are saying. I will take it into

consideration."

I cancel and reschedule the meeting with my staff. Lunch with Tinea zaps all creativity, emotions, and drive out of me.

I curl my leg beneath me on the couch. The merlot slithers down my throat. I eye the remaining bottle on the coffee table.

I'm finishing you tonight.

Damn, Tinea. She's right. I am not in love with Sam, but I do love him. Is it a necessity to be in love with someone before marrying them? Can't you just have good feelings? How did she expect me to refuse his proposal in front of everyone? That would have been cruel. Hell, he is Samuel Dixon, one of the top centers in the country. Many women around the country would run me over to be with him.

I eye the six-carat, halo, emerald cut, diamond ring sitting on top of my ring finger. I down the remaining merlot from my glass. I grab the bottle from the coffee table, turning the bottle to my head.

Sam and I work perfectly. We both have careers that keep us pretty busy. Between the pre-season, twenty-six-week regular basketball season, road trips, and practices, we see each other sparingly. He's brought up the idea of us moving in together a couple times. Moving in with Sam is not an option. The thought of me being homeless if we broke up makes us moving in together a deterring factor.

It's either the empty bottle of merlot or reality that smacks me. I don't want to move in with Sam, I don't want to start a family with him, I don't want to marry him. I'm not in love with him.

It would be selfish of me to marry him.

I have to call it off.

Going to therapy the past two months has helped me a lot with dealing with the abandonment of my dad. My mom told me her side of the story, but I have never gotten my dad's side. I did call him that one time. Hearing the boy that answered the phone call him dad was too much for me.

Dr. Brooke, my therapist, recommended it would be beneficial to my healing process to write my dad a letter and mail it. I have started the letter five times. The furthest I have gotten is:

Hi Dad:

This is your forgotten daughter, Simone.

I delete it and promise myself I will write it another day. It's been a month, and still I can't get past the first line.

My therapist has helped me to see how I self-sabotaged my relationship with Ryan. Deep down, I knew that, but having my actions analyzed has me cringing most of our sessions.

The lucid images I have at night while lying in my bed alone. The adoration Ryan showed me. How willing he was to walk away from his mother for me.

Dr. Brooke points out my own father walked away from his family for my mother, but later left her. Seeing the pattern in my relationship with Ryan, I go into protective mode. The only way I know how to protect myself is to bail on it. She shows me how I projected my feelings for my dad onto Ryan.

Each time I leave my session with Dr. Brooke, a heavy weight goes home with me. I ruined the chance to have a life with the man that I love. I chose the door of fear instead of living life.

Life is like the matrix. You are given a blue pill and a red pill; right or left. Your choice determines your future. I took the wrong pill.

If only I could go back in time.

The Rhodes Agency believes in healthy competition. The creative directors compete in house for each possible new account. There are four creative directors, and my biggest competition is Alex. There is a buzz going around the office of a new account The Rhodes Agency has been trying to land for the past ten years.

Today I'm wearing a black pencil skirt, and a purple sleeveless silk shirt that matches with my black, Prada, peep-toe shoes. I feel unstoppable. My team and I have this campaign in the bag.

We sit at the conference table, eager to learn about the company's account we are vying to attain. Upper management has been tight lipped about who the company is.

The room goes silent when Christopher Strongarm, the president, and Sylvia Rhodes, the owner and CEO, enter the conference room. I'm shocked to see Sylvia Rhodes.

Chris sits to the right of Sylvia, who sits at the head of the table. They waste no time and get right to it.

"I know that everyone is eager to learn about the new account. First, let's get an update on your current campaigns." His lips are pinched, eyes dark with a serious demeanor.

We spend the next thirty minutes reviewing accounts and providing next steps.

"Next, we have been soliciting this company for the past ten years with no luck. They normally work with CLP, LLC—Clifford, Leeward and Parker—but they are looking for fresh eyes. Has anyone seen the new building on 38th and 5th?" Chris asks, surveying the room.

"Yeah, the Mulligan Group is the architect," Roger answers.

"All the buildings they design are exceptional, but this one is extra special. These condominiums are also owned by the Mulligan Group, and they reached out to us to market it."

My breathing stops. My heart plummets.

"The point person at the Mulligan Group will be …"

Please don't say, Ryan. Don't say Ryan. I chant.

"Andrew Stillic. I want presentations ready in one week. Since they are looking for a couple options, I will pick the best two to present to Andrew."

I jot down the information with mixed emotions. Excitement at the possibility of winning the account. Afraid to run into Ryan.

I need to talk with Dr. Brooke about this.

"Lastly, Mrs. Rhodes has an announcement."

I peer at Sylvia, interested in what she has to say. She never attends our weekly meetings; this must be important.

She drums her fingers on the table.

"I have been the head of this company for the past forty-five years. It's time for me to enjoy time with my family. Effective immediately, there will be a new CEO of Rhodes Agency." She beams.

In walks a man dressed in a tailored navy suit. He flicks an invisible piece of lint from his jacket. The corner of his mouth curves up.

He looks familiar.

Chris's face hardens. This pompous ass thought he was going to be CEO.

I chuckle.

"I am happy to introduce you to my son, James Goodman."

A memory filters through my brain—a face with the same forget-me-not blue eyes.

My mouth hangs open.

My chest compresses. My body starts to quake. My hands become clammy.

It can't be.

My eyes roamed over his facial features again. I shake my head, trying to clear out the cloud in my brain.

He looks like the picture.

I excuse myself from the room. I run, bursting into the ladies' restroom. I lean over the sink on the brink of a panic attack.

I know that face. It's the face of the man I have wondered about my entire life.

It's my dad.

I lean against the wall, shaken by my realization. I cup my face and bawl.

Chapter Thirty-Five

I wash my face, wiping every inch of makeup I meticulously applied this morning off. I pull my shoulders back and look into the mirror. The broken, little girl stares back at me.

I have to see Dr. Brooke today.

I give myself a couple more minutes to gather the energy I need before returning to my meeting. Christopher will most likely request for me to meet with him afterward to chastise me for walking out.

I walk into an empty conference room. My notepad I left behind is gone. I head to my office in a daze.

I sit behind my desk, unlock my computer, and gaze at the screen.

Dr. Brooke.

I retrieve my cellphone and send a text to Dr. Brooke explaining my dilemma.

I fold my arms and lay my head upon my desk.

"Excuse me, Simone?" Rachel interrupts my solace.

I slowly lift my head and try to smile.

"What's up?" My voice wavers.

"Roger dropped your notepad off. He said not to worry, you didn't miss anything." She places the notepad and pen on the desk.

"Thanks."

"Are you okay?" A hint of worry lines her face.

"I'm good."

"Okay, I will just be at my desk if you need me."

She retreats to her desk.

My phone chimes. Dr. Brooke will be available to see me at six. It's only 3:41. I wake up my computer and type a quick email to my team and Mr. Strongarm, informing them that I would be out of the office for the remainder of the day. I compose another email addressed to my team with a list of tasks I expect to have completed when I get back in the office tomorrow.

I grab my purse and jacket from the coat hanger in the corner.

"Ms. Goodman, where do you think you are going?" Mr. Strongarm steps through the doorway.

Oh my gosh, Chris is such a pain in the ass.

"I am not feeling well. I am on my way out. I did send you an email." I glare at him.

"It was unprofessional of you to walk out of the meeting. You gave Mr. Goodman a bad first impression."

I freeze. "Did he say that?"

"Not in so many words."

He can go to hell.

"Well, hopefully I can change his impression of me in the future." I lean back against my desk. "Anything else before I go?"

"No, no." He waves me off like an insignificant bug. "Can't wait to see what your team comes up with for the Mulligan campaign." He smirks.

Christopher is an opportunist. He tramples on anyone or anything to get what he wants. Our weekly meetings are daunting. He is monotonous. He barks his orders all the time and believes his ideas are always the best. I thought he was a shoe in for CEO when Mrs. Rhodes retired. I am happy she chose differently.

"It will be good." I bob my head.

He studies me from head to toe, stroking his chin.

I gave him a fixed glare.

"See you bright and early tomorrow." He turns and leaves.

Such an ass

"What did you feel when you saw him?" Dr. Brooke asks.

"What did I feel? What didn't I feel should be the question," I reply.

Her brow raises, waiting for me to answer the question. We go through this each time. I answer her question with a question. She waits for me to gather my thoughts and give an actual answer.

I take a deep breath. "Disbelief, fright, anger, sadness, longing." I play with frills on the pillow.

"What does each emotion represent?" She scribbles on her notepad.

"Disbelief that it was actually him in the flesh. He was standing there. I could see him. Fright because he is now the CEO. Will I be able to continue working at the company? What would the work dynamic be with him around every day?" I pause. "Anger. I am angry that he left me and never looked back. I am angry that I long for my father's love and attention. I am angry that I have let this man affect my life." Tears rain down my face. I smash the pillow to my chest. "I am sad … I am saddened by the entire situation." I press the pillow to my face and scream on top of my lungs.

"You know what the worst part is? My boss Christopher told me that James' impression of me is not that great."

Dr. Brooke cocks her head to the side. "How did hearing that make you feel?"

"I am bearing all my emotions today, aren't I?" I sigh. I meet her gaze. "That's why I felt sad. I wanted him to see a strong woman who has been able to accomplish a lot without his fucking guidance and help. Instead, he wasn't impressed."

She gives me a confused look. "How do you know that's how he feels?"

"That's what Chris said. He got a bad first impression."

"You are looking at the situation emotionally instead of objectively. Did your father say that you are not a strong, accomplished woman? You are assuming it's the way he feels without any proof."

I shrug. *I guess she's right.*

"Are you planning on working tomorrow?"

"Yeah."

"What's your plan?"

"That's why I'm here. So, you can tell me what to do," I snap at her.

"Talk with him. This may bring you some closure."

She's lost her mind. I couldn't write a letter, but I am going to talk to him face to face?

I shake my head. "I don't know if that is going to happen, Dr. Brooke."

"I believe it's the best thing."

I can see myself going into his office, yelling at the CEO, then getting fired. Not happening.

"Your coffee is on your desk," Rachel mentions as I walk by her desk that sits outside of my office.

"Thanks, Rach. Can you check if the conference room is available at 11? If it's available, reserve it for three hours, and send an email to the team." I give her my American Express card. "Call Charlie's and have them bring bunch."

"Got it, Simone."

"Thanks, Rachel."

The cells in my body welcome the warmth of the mocha. As the heat spreads through me, my tensed muscles begin to loosen up. I enter the building petrified of running into James. I can't keep looking over my shoulder every minute afraid of running into him or of him showing up in my office.

I'm going to have to find a new job. This sucks. Besides my issues with Chris and Alex, I really love working here.

I have to start searching for a job soon, but until then I need to prepare for my meeting.

"Rach," I call out.

"Yes."

I look up and see her standing in the doorway. "Can you please go down and get the mockup board for the Peterson campaign from Ashley?"

I review the PowerPoint presentation while waiting for Rachel to return.

Although my job description has me taking on a more managerial role, I still like to dip my feet back in the trenches, helping my team with ideas and staying late hours at night overcoming roadblocks. It also helps when you have an amazing team.

"Good morning." I sit next to Ashley, one of the two graphic designers on the team. "First let's go over the mockup board and presentation for Peterson."

"Let's get the date corrected and change the background for the billboard to a dusty mauve. We can reach out to Mark at Peterson's and set a date and time for the presentation. Great job, everyone." I clap and the team joins in.

Robert starts to shimmy. "I heard about the account we are going to win."

"That building is sleek. I love the name Avec Amour," Ashley says in a French accent.

"We have one week to complete presentations for Chris. He will pick the two he feels matches the Mulligan brand. From there, the two teams will present to Andrew Stillic." I smile. "Any ideas?"

"We need to get inside the building, see the aesthetics, the layout, the finishes, the appliances," Robert answers.

"Great idea. Rachel, please reach out to Andrew and set an appointment for us to get access to the building. Also, see if he will be able to meet with us there. We can pick his brain."

"They are selling the condominium so we need to have print ad and web design concepts prepared," Ashley chimes in.

"We need to get into the building ASAP. Don't make any plans for the next couple days. We are going to be working long hours," I warn.

"If there aren't any other matters to discuss, the meeting is adjourned." I stand and start to gather my things.

"Perfect timing," an unfamiliar voice booms behind

me. "I get to meet all of you at once."

The voice walks to the center of the room. His face comes into view. James Goodman.

God, I thought you would have given me more time.

I watch him as he greets each person. He seems soft and understated. I smile at my team as they nervously introduce themselves.

A blazing furnace of emotions dwells in me, itching to burst out. I bring the bottle of cold water to my mouth. I have to maintain my composure. I am a professional if nothing else.

"And you must be Miss Goodman. I wasn't able to meet with you yesterday. If you have a couple minutes, can you meet with me in my office?" His forget-me-not blue eyes warm as he looks at me.

"Sure thing, Mr. Goodman. Let me put away my documents, and I can meet you in ten minutes." I force a smile.

"Nice meeting you all. I look forward to getting to know you." He strolls out of the room.

"That was nerve wracking," Ashley breaths aloud.

"You guys handled yourselves great. Let's get the Peterson account wrapped today and start working on ideas for the Mulligan account."

I walk briskly to my office—a safe space for me to deflate and prepare my mind and soul to have a conversation with James.

"Simone," Rachel calls out as I walk past her desk. "Mr. Dickson call—"

I put up my hand. "Not right now."

I walk into my office, and lock the door. I anxiously pace the floor. Dr. Brooke believes talking with James will help me to garner closure. How will I even broach the issue? He hasn't seen me in over twenty-five years. In all honesty, he doesn't know who I am. He wants to talk with his employee, not his long, lost daughter.

The clock on the wall ticks down like a timer on a bomb. I can't stop this meeting from happening. Each time the second hand moves, it lugs me anxiously forward.

I stop pacing.

You are freaking out for nothing, Simone.

I head out of my office and inform Rachel of my whereabouts.

"Hi, Misty, is Mr. Goodman available?" I ask his executive assistant.

"He's on a phone call. Go ahead and have a seat. I will let him know that you are here." She smiles.

"Thanks."

I sit down in the arm chair. My eyes roam around the waiting area. I revel in the beautiful paintings on the wall. I drum my fingers on my leg, anxiously waiting.

"Simone, you can go on in," Misty says.

I enter the office that once belonged to Mrs. Rhodes. I look around the room. All the years I have worked at this company, today is the first time I have set foot in this room. It boasts a clear view of the city, with an ornate desk in the middle of the room, a round table that seats four in the corner, and a brown leather couch. The white walls are bare of pictures or paintings. The room lacks personality.

He just got here, my inner voice chastises me.

"Go ahead and have a seat," He points to the chairs in front of his desk.

Ready or not.

I smile and take a seat.

"How are you doing today, Simone?"

"I'm doing well. How are you, Mr. Goodman?"

"Getting to know my employees before getting down to the real work."

"That's good. It helps when you know your staff." I slowly release a breath through my teeth.

"How do you like working here?"

He's going to fire me. Just great. Great.

"I love it. It's what I wanted since I was little. It brings me joy when I turn on the TV or walk down the street and see an ad and know that I had a hand in it."

"That's good." He smiles and nods.

I feel it, the anvil that preparing to drop.

"I was told that you have the Peterson's campaign."

I nod. "I do. We will be presenting the final product in a couple days."

"I would like for your team to run it by me first before presenting it."

What? He thinks I don't know what we are doing. I have been working with this client for two years.

I give a tight smile. "No problem, sir."

I squeeze my fingers together. We stare at each other in utter silence. I feel a soft panic grow the longer I sit here. His eyes look me over. He runs his hand across his face and releases a heavy breath.

"How's Rose?"

The anvil plummets with my heart attached. He knows who I am.

I jump from my seat.

"I can't do this with you here." I shake my head, walking toward the door.

"Simone, please." He stands. "Have dinner with me tonight?"

I look at his bewildered face.

Chapter Thirty-Six

"Dinner." Water wells in my eyes. "I can do dinner. When and where?"

"Tonight at 7 p.m. at the Oxford. Will that work?"

I nod in agreement.

Oxford is the restaurant for the pretentious. I hear the food is great, but good luck getting a reservation unless you're a socialite, politician, famous, or rich.

"How can I help you?" the snobby hostess asks. She looks at me as if I am standing in the wrong place.

I look down at my one shoulder, short, black, cocktail dress and black, strappy, Prada heels. I cock my head to the side and narrow my eyes. "I am meeting James Goodman."

"Oh yes, Mr. Goodman. Right this way." She smiles.

Bitch.

The hostess immediately escorts me to the back of the restaurant. James is seated in a secluded area. He stands upon seeing me. He pulls my chair out.

"Thank you," I say.

"You look beautiful."

"Thanks, Mr. Goodman."

"Mr. Goodman." He shakes his head. "You can call me James. Hopefully one day you will call me dad."

The waiter interrupts us and takes our order. I glance over at James. He smiles at me.

Calling him dad? That's a bit much. *Is he crazy? He*

was a dad for the first two years of my life.

James interrupts my inner monologue.

"I know that you calling me dad is a long stretch, but I am hopeful that one day we will be able to build our relationship to that level."

"So, you are here now seeking to have a relationship with me? Why now? What's the point?" I furrow my brows.

"Why not?" He puts his hands out. "I fucked up. I realized that the day I left the woman that I loved. I left her to—"

"You left her for money. That's why you left. You didn't give a damn about her or me. You didn't care at all," I whisper-yell. "You went on with your life: got married and had children. You replaced us." I point my finger at him.

"I didn't leave because of money. I left to protect you and your mom."

That's a shit of an excuse. I squeeze my eyes shut.

"You left to protect us? You did a great job at that. Mom worked multiple jobs before she got hired by the Mulligans and worked her way up to house manager." I look away. "I don't even know why I'm here," I muse. "I have wished for you for so long, and now that you are here, I still feel empty."

"I am sorry that I wasn't there. I can't erase the past, but we can work on our future. Please," he pleads.

"Why?" I wipe a tear from the corner of my eye.

"I love you. I want to make this right. I want to make us right."

I open my mouth to reply. James is saved from my sharp tongue when our meals arrive.

What the hell does he know about love? You love me? Is this dude for real? Sitting here telling me he loves me.

203

"Tell me, how did you end up working at Rhodes?" He cuts into his steak.

"I did a paper on the agency in college and fell in love with the brand and the type of work they do. I applied for a summer internship and was fortunate enough to land it. Got offered a full-time position after college and worked my way up from there."

Unlike Alex. Wait a minute.

Alexandra Goodman was Mrs. Rhodes' granddaughter. Is she James's daughter? *That would fucking suck.*

"Is Alexandra your daughter?" I ask, although I'm scared of the answer.

James laughs. "Good God, no! She's my niece. Your cousin. She is my older sister Jeanne's daughter."

I nod in understanding.

"When you are ready, I would like for you to meet your brother, Charles. He knows about you."

"He does?"

"Yeah, and he can't wait to meet you."

"Really." I swallow the anxiety building.

I cross my knife and fork over my plate. I lean forward and glare at James. "Tell me something. Why did you choose to speak with me today?"

He wipes his mouth with the napkin and throws it over his plate. "When I walked into that room yesterday and saw your face, I thought I was seeing a ghost. You look just like her. Your mom. Your eyes, your nose, the shape of your face. I look at you and I see her. After you left, I figured I might be on the right track. I asked Christopher for your name. I knew one hundred percent then that you were my daughter. I didn't want to waste time and create an uncomfortable work environment for us both. I decided to do what I long wanted and bit the bullet."

I burst out in laughter. "So, you didn't want to create an uncomfortable work environment for us. You knew I recognized you when I walked out of that meeting. It wasn't about me being uncomfortable. It's about you. It's always been about you." I point at him. My face hardens at the realization that this wasn't about him wanting a real relationship with me. "You know what …" I stand and walk out of the restaurant.

My apartment feels empty when I get home from dinner with James. The normal solace I feel when I get home has vanished. I grab my phone and send a 911 text to Tinea.

Ti: 911. Had dinner with my dad tonight, bring wine, lots of wine.

Thirty minutes later, my doorbell rings.

I roll over and slam my hand on the obnoxiously loud alarm. With my eyes closed, I stretch my hand onto the side table in search of my cellphone.

I peep with one eye at the time. "Ah." *I am not getting up.* The two bottles of wine swim around in my head. I fire off a quick email to Rachel and my team informing them that I won't be in today and that I will meet them at Avec Amor at 9: 15 a.m. for our meeting with Andrew of the The Mulligan Group.

I throw my phone with no care of where it lands, roll over in my bed, and let darkness cover me.

My head hangs, looking at my intertwined fingers as I sit on the fuchsia couch in Dr. Brooke's office located in her brownstone in Brooklyn.

How do I answer her question?

"I feel … He comes with his BS story andexpects me to welcome him with open arms. It's beenover twenty years. If he wanted to have a relationship with me, he could have searched for me years ago. Hehas the money and the resources. If this fucked up situation didn't present itself, I don't think I would have ever seen or heard from him. I didn't even know that Mrs. Rhodes is my grandmother. I don't think she knows who I am, or if she does, she doesn't care to get to know me."

"What do you want from him?" Dr. Brooke asks.

"What do you mean?" My brow wrinkles. "What do you think I want?" Dr. Brooke looks at me over her the glasses perched on her nose. They add a poise to her face.

She patiently waits for me to reply.

"Before, I yearned for him to be in my life, but now I'm conflicted. I mean, I've gotten this far withouthim. At this point, what value can he add to my life?"

"Do you feel that's the best option for you?"

"Do you think it's the best thing for me?" I reply, staring into her brown eyes. I pay her a lot of money to tell me what I should do, not for me to figure it out myself.

"It's not the best option for—?"

"Why the hell not? I can quit my job. I have some savings that can tide me over until I find a new one. I wouldn't have to deal with him at all then."

"You just answered why it isn't the best option. Until you deal with your emotional issues concerning your dad, the fear, depression, and anxiety you go through will continue to affect your ability to have any meaningful relationships with men. In order to heal, Simone, you must make peace with your relationship with him."

You know she's right. You've already lost Ryan because of your fears.

James needs to earn the right to have a relationship with me. This is not going to be as easy.

"I guess you are right. I want a relationship with my father. I'm just extremely angry." Within me still lives the little girl starved of the father's love she craves. That pain still lingers beneath, drowning my soul.

"You are justified in your feelings toward him. Healing will not happen overnight; you will need to take the necessary steps to accomplish this. You may want to invite him to a couple of our sessions."

I worry my bottom lip. An image of my mom comes to mind. I haven't told her about James yet. This will be a hard conversation to have with her. I will need to let her know before taking any other further steps with James. "That may be a good idea."

In preparation for the upcoming internal tug of war for the Mulligan account, Henry and Ashley, the graphic designers, Roger the art director, Marcus the copywriter, and I meet with Andrew Stillic at Avec Amor, the new condominium designed and built by the Mulligan Group.

Avec Amor—with love. I love the name. The building design is a seamless merger of classic and modern. Glass and stone.

"You must be, Simone," a dark, husky voice catches me off guard.

He is not what I expected at all. This guy is gorgeous, although not as hot as Ryan. He's dressed in he a slim fitting black suite, black shirt, and black tie. His brown hair is styled effortlessly low on the sides and rumpled on top.

Nice.

I stretch forward my hand. "Yes, Mr. Stillic, it's nice to meet you. Thank you for taking the time to meet with us today."

"No problem. Let me give you a tour."

We follow him to the elevators.

The eight-story building has four units on the first six floors; the penthouse occupies the two top floors.

There are tray ceilings in the master bedroom and crown molding throughout. The style is open concept with a two face, electric fireplace positioned between the kitchen and living room.

"The fireplace isn't wood burning?" Ashley gives a confused look.

Ashley and Roger snaps photos as we stroll through units.

"It's electric," Andrew replies.

I gasp as we walk into the penthouse. The first thing that catches my attention is the 360-degree view of the city, made possible by floor-to-ceiling glass walls. It sits at a total of 7,425 square feet. Four bedrooms, five bathrooms. Three bedrooms are on the second floor. The 1,100 square feet master bedroom with an ensuite. The bathroom has a soaking tub, double vanity, and steam shower.

His and hers walk-in closets. The woman's closet resembles a fancy boutique shop.

I could live in here.

The first-floor has an open plan living room, kitchen, and a separate room for a formal dining room. I turn around the corner from the kitchen and stop in my tracks.

This two-tier library.

The stairs to the right of the room leads to a circular shelf filled with books. A large, white sectional, and a rectangular, wood coffee table sits below. A chandelier hangs in the center of the room.

This room is whimsical.

"Who was the architect on this project?" I enquire.

"Mr. Mulligan," Andrew says with a knowing smile.

I smile. "Which one?"

"Ryan. You know them?"

"No. Do you have some extra time for us to pick your brain?"

He looks at his watch. "I can spare some time."

We discuss the design concepts, the company's targeted demographic, its brand, and the image the company wants to portray. The Mulligan Group is known as an architectural firm, not as real estate developers.

After our meeting with Andrew, we go back to the office and brainstorm some ideas for a print and digital campaign.

"Simone," I answer the phone.

"Did you meet with anyone from the Mulligan Group recently?" Chris barks through the phone.

"I did. I met with Andrew Stillic earlier today with the team. Why?"

"I don't know what you said or did, but I just got off the phone with Andrew and they want you to handle the campaign."

"Really? That's great, right?" I ask, confused by the harshness of his tone. Rhodes has been trying to get the Mulligans' account for a decade. Chris should sound more excited about this.

"I don't know how you were able to pull it off. Campaign presentation is within three weeks. Don't lose this account." He slams his phone.

I pump my fist. "Yes!" I shout.

"What happened?" Rach runs into the office.

"My team just landed the Mulligan project."

"Congratulations, boss. Early days and late nights?"

"Yep, we have three weeks to present. Reserve conference room B all day tomorrow."

Rachel gives me a high five and leaves.

Chapter Thirty-Seven

It's been a couple weeks since I have spoken to or seen James. I'm grateful to have my mind occupied with the Avec Amor campaign. I walk briskly to the executive suites before the pressure building on my chest suffocates me. Each step I take brings me closer to my resolution.

"Misty, is Mr. Goodman in his office?" I ask, passing James's executive assistant.

"Yeah, but Simone ..."

I barge into my dad's office, ignoring Misty's unimportant protestations.

He looks up from the papers on his desk, shocked by the intrusion and the intruder. I stand rooted by the door.

The office door flies open. "Sorry, Mr. Goodman. I was trying to let Simone know—"

"It's fine, Misty." James waves her out of the office. "Simone." James's stern voice echoes in the room.

"I have been going to therapy and I would like for you to join me tomorrow at 7:00 p.m. I will email you the address."

The crow's feet around his eyes crinkle as he laughs. His laughter is like a crashing wave that isn't joyful or pure.

"I don't need therapy. We just need to spend some time together," he states.

Anger bubbles deep in my innards; a raging sea of

hurt and anger. I allow myself to be wrapped in darkness, erupting in a maddened state. "Are you fucking kidding me? You self-righteous jerk!" I bellow, not caring if the entire floor can hear. "You are the reason why I'm in therapy. You are the reason why I lost the love of my life. Because of you, I have this crazy thought that no man will ever want to be with me." I tap my index finger against my temple. "I suffer with depression and anxiety because of you. I won't allow myself to fully love and be loved in return because of you. You told me a couple weeks ago that you love me, you did what you thought was best to protect us—crap, that you want a relationship with me. If you truly love me, then you will help me heal and show up tomorrow. If you don't, then fucking leave me alone."

As the last words escape me, I slowly emerge from the anger I possessed. I feel relief as I exhale loudly.

He sits back in his chair staring at me, stupefied.

"If you want a father-daughter relationship with me, this is what I require. Otherwise, we can continue being strangers. The ball is in your court. Have a good night, Mr. Goodman," I whisper and storm out of his office.

Later that night, I call my mom and tell her about my encounters with James. The love of her life. Not a sound can be heard on the other end of the line as I speak.

"Mom, are you still there?" I look at cellphone screen to verify we are still connected. "Mom."

She sniffles.

My heart crumbles at the sound of my mom in tears. I can only imagine the turmoil burrowing inside her soul. It hurts me that I am the one ripping open her emotional scars.

You had to tell her. It would have hurt her worse if you didn't.
"Mija, I will call you back."
"Sure, Mom."

Mom never called me back last night. I wish I was there to support her the way she always does for me whenever the demons of my missing father appear. I reach over from my bed and grab my cellphone and open the message screen to send my mom a text; to my surprise, there is an unread text from Mom.

MOM: Baby, I am so proud of you. You are such a beautiful and strong woman. I am okay with you wanting to have a relationship with your dad. It's time for you to heal. I pray that he shows up today. If he doesn't show up tonight, I'm here. Call me. Remember that I LOVE YOU ALWAYS.

A smile comes to my face at her words.
SIMONE: LOVE YOU MORE.

I slowly walk up the stairs leading to Dr. Brooke's office. Trepidation sizzles throughout me. If James doesn't show up, it will be the final nail in the coffin for the only man I have ever wanted to love. Water leaks from the corners of my eyes. I flick the unwanted tears away. I close my eyes as I rest my hand on the door handle.

You can do this, Simone. Inhale, exhale.

I push open the door. There sits James Goodman fidgeting on Dr. Brooke's couch.

Wow! Is this wunderland?

Chapter Thirty-Eight

Ashley, Roger, and I are escorted to a conference room inside the offices of the Mulligan Group. It's been almost six years since I have stepped foot inside these walls. We set up our presentation and take our seats, waiting for the Mulligan's team.

My stomach is tight, and my teeth lock together. Fear of seeing Ryan overcomes me. It's the chill of icy cold weather numbing my brain and only offering one thought. It's today.

This morning as I got dressed in a powder blue, bodycon, midi dress, an image of Ryan pops in my mind. A feeling rises inside, pushing me not to attend the presentation. Dread owns me in this moment, attempting to reverse my steps back.

I sit in the conference room, tapping my feet. My nerves are on fire.

Andrew and three other individuals walk into the conference room, taking a seat across from us.

"Sorry for keeping you waiting," Andrew says. "Whenever you are ready, you can begin."

I stand and walk to the front of the room, both happy and sad that Ryan is nowhere in sight.

Dr. Brooke has helped me to see that the feelings I have for Ryan will not end. They are embedded in my soul. It will not end until I cease to exist.

I begin the presentation, confident with the approach my team and I have come up with. I watch the nods and smiles from Andrew and his team.

Twenty minutes into my presentation, a weird chill runs through me. I shiver. My chest tightens. I turn, looking at the doorway, and come eye to eye with Ryan Mulligan.

I stutter and stumble at the sight of him.

"Sorry for the interruption," Ryan says as he walks to the other end of the conference table, pulls out the chair in the center of the table, and sits. "You may continue, Ms. Goodman." He smirks.

He has to sit there! He passes all those seats to sit there! He's trying to rattle me. Damn, it's working. Sexy motherfucka.

I shuffle the papers on the table, giving me time to collect myself.

Ryan studies me the entire meeting. He does not ask any questions or utter a single word. Each time I glance at him, his emeralds meet mine. I look away quickly and finish the presentation. Once the meeting is through, he gets up, looks at me, and winks before he walks out the door.

"Any other questions?" I ask.

"No. Give me a minute." Andrew steps out of the room.

We sit in uncomfortable silence, waiting for his return.

He walks back in five minutes later, smiling. "We love the ideas that you presented. Let's get it implemented."

I breathe a sigh of relief. "Thank you."

"No, thank you. You and your team did an exceptional job." We shake hands.

215

We gather our materials and make an appointment to meet again once the billboards and website design has been completed.

"Did you see Mr. Mulligan? He is hot." Ashley fans herself as we ride down on the elevator. "I wonder if he's single. He looks like a man that knows how to handle a woman in bed."

Roger groans.

I sigh. *Girl, if you only knew.*

"Completely unprofessional, Ashley. Get yourself together." I burst out laughing.

"There he goes." Ashley nudges me as we exit the Towers building that houses the Mulligan Group.

I look in the direction she's pointing to see Ryan and a woman enter the Mercedes parked in front of the building. A ping of envy strikes me.

That should be me with him. *Well, you fucked that up.*

Back at the office, I reanalyze today's encounter with Ryan. What was the purpose of him being at the meeting? He didn't say a word. Was he there to ensure his team was on point? Did he come just to rattle me? Did I get the account because of him? Who's the girl? How long have they been together? Did he like the way I looked? I sigh and run my hand through my newly colored blonde highlights.

As much as I've tried to tell myself that I didn't get dressed with Ryan in mind, I did. I wanted him to love what he saw. To crave me as much as I crave for him.

The clock reads 4:53 p.m. I stare at the excel sheet. I exhale. *This is a bust.* I send a text to Tinea and Jackie.

Ti & Jackie: Drinks at Peppers in 30!!!

I look up at the sound of a knock on my office door. I am surprised to see Andrew Stillic standing in my doorway.

"Hi." I stand. "Come on in." I point toward the chairs in front of my desk. "Have a seat." I sit after him.

"What do I owe this pleasure?"

"I was in the neighborhood and wanted to drop by."

My eyebrows rise.

"You guys did a great job on the campaign; all the units except for the penthouse sold."

"The penthouse didn't sell? I was sure it would have been the first to go. If I could afford it, I would take it."

"We're not worried about it." His eyes sift to one side as if pondering something. "Truthfully, I stopped by to ask if you would join me for dinner on Friday."

"What?"

"I waited until the campaign was over. I have been attracted to you since we met." He smiles. "So, what do you say dinner, Friday?"

"Yeah, why not?" I smirk.

"Great, I will leave and let you get back to your day. I will see you on Friday."

Chapter Thirty-Nine

The waiter pours us each a glass of pinot grigio, then places the bottle on the table.

"Are you ready to order?" the waiter, Tony, asks.

"Ah." I pick up the menu.

"Give us a couple minutes please."

I look at Andrew and smile shyly. I bite my lip; his eyes sparkle. I laugh and look away. I am conflicted being here. A big part of me feels I'm betraying Ryan. Another part of me is excited. I haven't been on a date in six months.

Is Andrew aware of me and Ryan's past?

Andrew is funny. I have been enjoying our conversation. It doesn't hurt that he's easy on the eyes.

"How long have you worked for the Mulligans'?"

"Four years. I met Ryan while he attended graduate school at Harvard."

"Oh. Of course, you Harvard men stick together." I wink.

He laughs. "Most times."

"Are you hungry?"

"Starving. I didn't eat all day so that I could fit in this dress." I laugh.

"The dress looks amazing on you, if I may say so myself." He licks his lips.

"Oh stop." I wave him off, laughing. "Really don't stop. You are good for a girl's ego." We laugh.

We place our orders. Should I tell him about Ryan

and I? I am having a great time with Andrew. If I tell him, I risk the mood changing. I don't want to ruin the date. We talk about our favorite music, bands, and singers.

"Stop it." I burst out in laughter. My head falls back.

"Hey, Ryan." Andrew sounds confused. "I didn't know you were coming here tonight?"

My laughter dies. I look to Ryan standing next to my chair, his hands in the pockets of his pants. I pinch my eyes together, leering at him. A rush of adrenaline hits me, forgetting that Andrew is sitting across from me.

His jaw tenses as he glares at me. Without saying a word, he stretches forth his hands toward me. Without any words being spoken, I know what he's asking. My chest thumps to the hard beats of my heart. It's as if Travis from blink 182 is using my heart as a drum.

Without much thought, I take his hand and stand.

"Andrew, I am sorry about this," Ryan says. We leave hand in hand.

We stand outside the restaurant waiting for the valet to bring his car. His grip on my hand tightens as if he's scared I might flee. A dark Mercedes pulls up in front of us. Ryan opens the passenger door, guides and buckles me into the seat.

We sit in the car in silence. Guilt washes over me. *You are one messed up bitch. How could you have left that man sitting there like that?*

"Where are we going?" I ask, breaking the uncomfortable silence.

He turns toward me, his jaw clench; flames of anger stare at me. He looks back at the road. No answer given.

He turns into a garage, parks his Mercedes, and

switches off the ignition. He takes a breath, then looks over at me.

"Why would you do that?" he growls.

I gasp and point to myself. "Are you talking to me!?"

"Why do that?" He runs his hand over his face.

"Do what?"

He leans over the console. I feel his breath on my face. "My employee! Of all the people to date, my employee and friend."

"You're upset that I went on a sort-of-date you ruined with, Andrew. So, what?" I throw my hands out.

"So, what?" he shouts. "How could you consider sleeping with him?"

"WOW! Wait a minute. Going on a date with someone doesn't mean it will lead to sex," I yell. "How did you come to that conclusion?"

"Do you have any idea what it was like to listen to him gush over you? I sat there listening to him and pretending that the date was a great idea. When all I wanted to do was rip his fucking head off." He sits back, closing his eyes. "Did you say yes to get to me?"

"What!?" I shout. "Get over your fucking self."

He gets out of the car. I watch as he prowls around to the passenger door and opens it.

"Let's go," he demands.

"Go where?"

"Get out of the car, Simone!"

"The only place I want to go is home."

"You are such a fucking pain in my ass. Get the hell out of the car."

He's lost his ever-fucking mind. I sit, refusing to move. He can go to hell. We stare at each other, neither of us giving an inch.

"I want to go home." He shakes his head, lets out a heavy breath, and yanks me from the car. The door slams behind me. He heads toward the elevator.

I pull away. "What the hell, Ryan? Take me home."

He stalks back to me. I back up, scared by the cold look in his eyes. I'm squeezed between him and his car.

"What are you doing? Back up."

"Why did you leave the restaurant with me?"

My head goes down. "What? I don't have time for your games, Ryan. Take me home."

"Look at me." He lifts my chin. "You could have told me no. You could have stayed with Andrew."

"Would you have taken no for an answer?" I left with him because he's the man I love. The only man I desire.

"No," he says firmly. He brushes his thumb across my bottom lip. "You drive me crazy." He bends, capturing my mouth, tugging on my bottom lip.

"And you drive me insane." I wrap my hands around his neck as I press my body against his and kiss him. My tongue slips into his mouth. I growl. His kiss is eager with a sense of urgency.

He pulls away and chuckles.

"Let's go before I take you in this garage."

We walk hand in hand to the elevator. He enters a code and presses P. The door opens, and I gasp loudly. We are standing in the living from of the penthouse at Avec Amor.

"You kept it."

"Yeah, couldn't part with it. I designed it with you in mind."

I attack him.

221

We lay in bed, our limbs intertwined together. I am sated and happy.

Ryan lazily runs his hand through my hair. "Let's go to the Hamptons."

"We can go in the morning." I yawn.

"Let's go now."

"Now!" There's the spontaneity I love. I sit up on the bed. "Let's go. I will need to stop by my apartment and grab some clothes." I lean over and place a chaste kiss to his lips.

"For what?" All trace of humor vanishes.

"To wear."

"You won't be needing any clothing. We are not going to be leaving the house. More pointedly, you will hardly leave the bed."

"Really, now? Mr. Mulligan has become Mr. Kinky." I wink. "We won't leave the house?"

He shakes his head.

I jump off the bed and get dressed. Ryan follows suit.

It was 2:00 a.m. Saturday morning when we leave the city. The roads are quiet. I weirdly miss the noise of the daily hustle and bustle.

"I'm not going to let you slip through my fingers this time," Ryan states out of the blue.

"You're not?" My smile widens.

"Every time we are together, something happens and you run. I let you run. Not this time, Ms. Goodman. This time, it's forever. How do you feel about that?"

I don't know what to say. I turn and stare out the window. Forever. That word seems impossible to me when it comes to him. I have learned from Dr. Brooke that I have to face things and not be scared to love.

These past couple of months, the relationship with my dad and I has grown. I have gotten to know him better. The broken pieces have sealed. My brother, Charles, is a riot. I never thought I would enjoy being a big sister. James and I still go to lunch or dinner weekly, and Charles joins us when possible. My mom is happy that I am able to build a relationship with him. The two have even spoken a couple times.

My heart speeds with the simple thought of forever. I leave his question unanswered.

Midday Saturday midday finds me in a blissful state. Exhausted but sated. Sex with Ryan is heady. My core quivers of the thought of how right he feels inside me.

Oh crap! We have been having sex without any condoms. I'm not on any contraception.

I nervously bite my lip. I freeze in the kitchen with an egg in my hand. I gaze outside at the ocean. *I could get pregnant.*

Holy shit! I have to say something to him. We were so caught up in our emotions we forgot to use common sense.

"Come back to me," a voice whispers in my ear behind me.

"Shit!" I jolt; the egg cracks on the wooden floor. I grab a few paper towels, and bend over to clean up the mess.

I feel his fingers slowly rub over my sensitive clit. I inhale. I begin to rise and am instantly push back into position.

"Don't move," he growls.

223

I groan at the pleasurable assault. His two fingers fucks me hard while he presses his thumb on my clit.

"Don't stop, baby. Don't stop," I plead. That welcoming feeling builds inside and sweeps me into a different hemisphere. I slowly stand as the tremors begin to dissipate.

"Good morning, baby."

I turn to him and watch as he licks his fingers that were deep inside me clean. I stand on the tip of my toes to kiss his soft pillow lips. He picks me up. I wrap my legs around his waist as he carries me to the living room couch.

He slowly unbuttons my shirt.

"I always love watching you wear my shirts. I love taking them off even more."

I cannot believe we had sex again without any condoms.

Fuck.

"Babe, what's wrong?"

"What do you mean what's wrong?" I snap. He gives me the deer in headlights look. "We've been having sex without any form of protection." I push him off of me.

He sits up. "I don't get what the issue is? The sex is great."

"Yeah, I'm not worried about the sex. I'm worried about getting pregnant." I stand in front of him.

He pauses. A huge smile spreads across his face.

What the hell is he smiling about?

"That would just mean you couldn't run. We would be bonded together, forever." He kisses my stomach.

Suddenly he lifts me and slams me down on his erected dick.

"Ah!" I scream. He holds my waist as he pounds

hard into me.

"I can't wait for you to have my baby," he moans. "Marry me, Simone."

My head lulls back as I ride him into bliss.

I lay across the bed, wrapped in a towel after showering, in post coital afternoon bliss. Ryan cuddles me. I have had more sex this weekend than I have had in the past six years. We both can't get enough of each other. If we touch each other, we are going to fuck. I am happily tired and sore.

You're in wunderland.

He kisses my shoulder. "You never answered my question," he says softly, trailing kisses along my collar.

"What question?"

"Be mine forever."

There's that word again: forever. *Girl, stop being stupid. This man loves you. You love him. Stop being scared. You have nothing to be scared of now.*

"Why are you shaking? You're cold?"

Honesty is the best policy. "The word forever gets me nervous."

He taps my jaw. "Look at me."

"Yeah." I see the hurt and rejection he's feeling.

"You don't want to be with me?"

"Why would you think that?" I cup his face. "No."

"So, what's the issue?" He pulls away and sits up. I follow. I feel his glare. I refuse to meet his gaze.

"Stop looking away from me. Just be honest and talk."

I look back at him. "You don't want to marry me," he states. A dagger pierces my heart at the sound of the sadness in his voice.

"When did you hear me say that?"

"You are not answering the question, so it only leaves one conclusion."

"I'm just nervous, Ryan."

"What!" He laughs. "Why? You know that I love you and always will."

"I know, but your family will never approve."

"Fuck my mom. I've told you all my life I don't live for her."

You can't use your dad as an excuse anymore. Bitch, just dive on in. He is your wunderland.

"Simone, I love you." He gets off the bed, taking me with him. He abruptly drops down to one knee.

Oh my gosh … he is proposing to me butt ass naked.

"Simone Goodman. Sim. I have loved you since I was seventeen, and I love you still."

I laugh, wondering what movie he stole those lines from.

"I will never leave you. You are home for me. You took my heart and never gave it back. Will you put me out of my misery and say that you will be my wife?"

Tears stream down my face. I look at this beautiful man kneeling before me and know with him is where I'm meant to be.

"Yes."

"YES?"

"Yes, I will marry you any day."

He picks me up and twirls me around. "She said yes." He smiles, tracing kisses along my face.

He lays me back on the bed.

THE END

226

Epilogue

I lie in bed, rubbing my swelling belly. I look at my husband, Ryan, as he prepares for his day with glee. It's crazy how fast things spiraled since our weekend together in the Hamptons seven months ago.

The Sunday night after we returned from the Hamptons, Ryan and I didn't want our time to end. I grabbed a couple of items from my house, planning on spending a couple more days with him. A couple days turned into weeks, and weeks, into three months. I never lived in my apartment again.

Ryan has been working late these days. Avec Amor was such a big success he decided to build another luxury condominium. Saturdays are normally our leisure days, but there was an issue at the construction site so he left early this morning to oversee it. After he left, I went back to sleep for a few extra hours.

I walk into the kitchen wrapped in my fuchsia robe with the primary goal of inhaling a cup of coffee. My stomach lurches at the smell of the brew, and I make it to the bathroom just in time to release the remains of last night's Thai food. I heave and heave until there is nothing left in my stomach. I wrap a pile of toilet paper in hands, wiping at my mouth.

What the hell was that about? The food must had been bad.

Coffee rejected, and grumpy, I jog upstairs to complete my morning routine. I am attacked with a continuous wave of nausea during my shower, compounding my misery.

"Babe, Sim? Where are you?" Ryan yells; the sound of his boots echoes on the wooden floor.

Ryan finds me wrapped in a duvet curled on our bed.

"Hey, baby, what's wrong?" he asks. "I saw that you made coffee. I brought you up a cup just the way you like it."

"Get that away from me," I growl, as my stomach begins to lurch and gurgle. "Oh, gosh, not again." I swing my feet to the floor, rushing inside of ourensuite.

Ryan begins rubbing my back while I hug the toilet bowl. I shrug my shoulder, pushing Ryan's hands away. "No, just leave. I don't want you to see or smell this."

"I am not leaving." He hands me a cup of water to rinse my mouth.

I gurgle the liquid, washing out my mouth. I flush the contents of the toilet, then slouch onto the bathroom floor. I can't find the strength to walk back to the bed. I wrap my hands around Ryan's shoulders as he lifts me off the floor.

"Let me get you some soup."

"No." My voice is raspy from the constant cough. "I just want to sleep."

The vomiting persists the entire weekend, my stomach unable to hold on to any substance.

"I made a doctor's appointment, with Dr. Beck," Ryan informed me. How many people have their doctor's cellphone number?

Ryan and I sit in the Dr. Beck's office waiting patiently on the results of a couple of tests that he ran during my examination.

Dr. Beck walks into his office, and I assess his

demeanor to see if he is concerned.

I got nothing.

"Simone, when was the last time you had your period?" Dr. Beck asks.

I squint, trying to recall the information. "It's been three weeks."

"Three weeks?"

Ryan tenses. "What's wrong?"

"Nothing is wrong, Ryan. Simone is just pregnant."

"What?" I yell. "That can't be possible."

"Why not?" Dr. Beck ask.

"I have not missed my period at all," I say, bewildered.

"It's not uncommon for women to still see their periods while being pregnant during their first trimester. Come with me down to the ultrasound room. I can take a look and see how far along you are."

I turn, looking at Ryan's dimples staring back at me. We follow Dr. Beck, and I lay back on the table. Cold, gel liquid hits my stomach. Dr. Beck rubs a wand along the gel.

"Let's see what we got here," he says.

Our eyes are all glued to the screen.

"There is the sac with your baby." Dr. Beck continues to move the wand around. "Your uterus looks good. By my calculations, you are twelve weeks pregnant. Let's check the baby's heartbeat."

My soul leaps at the steady thumping sound. Ryan leans over me, looking at the screen in awe. He places a quick kiss on my lips.

"Thank you. I never thought you could have made me any happier than you did the day you agreed to marry me," Ryan declares.

"You're welcome," I say with a chaste kiss to his

lips.

"You need to get in contact with your OBGYN, Simone, and make an appointment."

"Will do, doctor." Ryan says.

First trimester. I am pregnant with Ryan's child.

Dr. Beck gives us a couple samples of prenatal vitamins to try. I can let my OBGYN know which one I prefer once we meet. We also get two ultrasound pictures of our little bean.

"We are not waiting to get married," Ryan says on our way back home.

"What? I can't plan a wedding now."

"We are getting married before the baby gets here."

"The baby is due in May. That only gives us less than six months. I'm not going to waddle down the aisle."

"You have less than six months. You have two."

"Are you crazy?" I screech. "You want to get married in January?"

"We don't need to plan anything elaborate. It can be very small and intimate. You, me, our parents, and close friends. That's it."

I scoff. "Yeah, give your mom another reason to hate me. She was already pissed when you told her we were engaged. She simmered down after a month and started the wedding planning. You can call and tell her about this change."

"I will." He removes my hand from his thigh, kisses it, and places it back.

Christina Mulligan softens toward me after learning she will be a grandmother. As if a light bulb finally got screwed in correctly and she could see how to get out of the wilderness. She emerges a better version of herself, casting away her poison of cynicism.

Ryan and his mom argue daily about our December 31st wedding date.

"Mom. What do you not understand? We are not changing the wedding date."

I shake my head listening to the daily back and forth between those two.

"Mom, fifty people. That's it. No more ... I don't give a flying hoot about other people's feelings ... It's not the company's wedding, it's mine ... Yes, I will be CEO one day ..." He exhales and hands me the phone. "I can't deal with this." He walks off.

I put the phone to my ear. "Hi, Christina."

"Hi dear," she says, sounding exasperated. "Can you believe that son of mine? I mean, the Rogers have known him since he was a baby. "

I sympathize with her. "I know. He's headstrong, and you know him better than me. Once he has his mind made up, there is no changing it. I can try talking to him," I lie.

"Will you do that? I just want to invite ten more people."

"Will do."

"Well, how are you feeling today?"

"Better."

It has been a crazy month since we found out that I was pregnant. Unable to keep much down, I have lost ten pounds instead of gaining weight. Mrs. Mulligan calls me daily to check in.

On New Year's Eve, I place my hand on my stomach,

looking at myself dressed in a white, A-line gown, with draping wrapped around the heart-shaped bodice and a swirly, frothy, draped skirt. The gorgeous gown is classic and sensual. I feel I'm in wunderland.

"Don't you mess up that makeup with your tears," Tinea cries out.

"I can't help it. It's the baby."

"Don't blame my grandchild." Mrs. Mulligan crinkles her eyes and nose.

"You look gorgeous, Mija," Mom exclaims. A knock sounds from the door. Jackie opens it and in walks in my dad.

"Hey, baby girl, he's impatiently waiting for you."

I am ready.

I ride in a Bentley with mom and dad to St. Patrick's Cathedral. Our nuptials are a traditional service. Lush, white flowers with greenery line the pews.

I stand in arm with my dad staring down the aisle at the emerald-eyed boy I have loved all my life, watching him as tears roll down his cheeks. I can't get to him fast enough.

Acknowledgments

I am still in disbelief that this is finally happening. Screams.

To my husband and our three musketeers. I want to thank you for giving me the time needed to finish this novel and encouraging me each step.

To mom, dad, D'wayne and Mark. Thanks for loving me and supporting me through this process. Pushing me not to give up and to continue on.

To Jon, my baby brother what can I say, but thank you, thank you. You provided my favorite chapter. Thanks for the love and continued support.

To Shannon, my sister, and best friend. The encouragement you have given me. The honest feedback that you provided throughout this process made me better. If it wasn't for your encouragement Wunderland wouldn't have seen the light of day.

It takes a village to write and publish a book. I want to thank my village, Pauline-editor, Angy-cover designer, Savannah-formatting, and Grey Promotions.

To my readers I hope you enjoyed Simone and Ryan's story as much as I do.

Forever Thankful,
Scar.

About the Author

Scarlett Se Leva, worked in banking for over 20 years. In 2019, after giving birth to her third child she made the decision to walk away and pursue her passion as a writer. Scarlett aka Scar has been a storyteller since the age of fourteen; you would find her sitting on the veranda in Jamaica with a pen and paper. She enjoys writing unexpected, steamy, suspenseful romance.

Scar resides in Florida with her husband and three daughters. When Scar isn't busy penning another story, you can find her with the family watching movies, playing dominoes, drinking wine or curled up in a corner with a book.

She loves getting to know her readers, so subscribe to her www.scarlettselevabooks.com, or friend her on Facebook www.facebook.com/scarlettselevabooks, or follow her on Twitter @letshavemocha.

Made in the USA
Columbia, SC
19 July 2021